Events of the Day

Events of the Day

A Tragedy of the American Sixties

Richard Swanson

Writers Club Press
New York San Jose Lincoln Shanghai

Events of the Day
A Tragedy of the American Sixties

Writers Club Press
an imprint of iUniverse.com, Inc.

For information address:
iUniverse.com, Inc.
5220 S 16th, Ste. 200
Lincoln, NE 68512
www.iuniverse.com

Cover design by Elizabeth Roherty; cover photo, Bruce Fritz

ISBN: 0-595-01070-9

Printed in the United States of America

For Fan, with continuing love and admiration

Acknowledgments

A number of caring manuscript readers helped bring this book into being: Natalie Aragno, Sue Bauman, Joel Carlson, Bill Feeny, Barbara Harris, Phil Martin, Jerry Minnich, Kay VanHorn and Larry Wilson. Betsy Roherty's graphic talents mirrored their insights, and to all these people my grateful thanks.

Contents

Washington, D.C., 1970, The White House

They've roused him from well-earned slumber, the FBI people. He's going to be tested again, called upon to lead!

All day yesterday, his aides were counseling moderation, while the press, that corps of sniveling conspirators, tried to rattle him again. The President is an extremist, blah, blah, blah. But he held firm as always. He knew who they really were, all of them on both sides: the liberal opposition's goon squads, and his ulcer-stomached allies. He's slept soundly, knowing that he stood right, didn't back away from the brawl.

At dinner last night, just the two of them, he told Pat to stay the course with him, that history would prove him a visionary. Over a fine '62 Bordeaux he tried out some of the phrases he was tinkering with, for his coming memoirs, while she sat politely stupefied. Earlier he was going to hint to the waiter, Eliot, to bring the wine glass by glass, but she'd ordered that the bottle be beside her—gotten to the servants before he had. Well, that was okay. Better not to have a tiff with her, about her habit, that would eventually float up in some sewage drain column about him. Enemies were everywhere, over there in China pulling Ho Chi Minh's strings, in the whining leftist caucuses of Congress, in the Catholic bishops fomenting distrust of him in their homilies, in the spoiled-brat agitators occupying the republic's streets, maybe even in the once-good people who served him and the First Lady dinner. Who could you trust these days but yourself?

Dear dimmed Pat. She wandered to bed right after dinner, or at least he thought so, not being sure of where her nocturnal wanderings took her these days. They'd stopped sharing the same bed years ago when his wrath in pitch-black hours would bolt him out of the sheets and covers.

Their isolation from one another, it's simply a cost for his greatness, he tells himself.

In his bathrobe he receives the FBI people. Steady as you go, his demeanor says. I'm President Nixon, there'll be no compromise with criminals, and J. Edgar Hoover and I understand one another. We own this government. We'll protect it.

They brief him. At a large university in The Midwest there's been a bombing of a campus building, which housed a U.S. Army math research facility, the target of student protests for years.

Campus infiltrators warned Hoover something like this might happen. With student unrest at the boil, after Cambodia and Kent State, the odds of something dramatic were increasing.

There are no leads yet. The bomb blew only an hour ago.

Agents have been alerted for additional revolutionary activity across the country.

Yes, he says, this could be the attempted national takeover. I saw this coming, heard it in the whisperings. *Nixon, your man, knew! All along!*

"The whisperings?" one of Hoover's assistants inquires. The underling doesn't understand, just doesn't see the obvious, that the word doesn't need explanation.

"Yes, the whisperings!"

They show him the pictures, setting aside their bafflement, their inadequacy. That's why he's president and they're foot-soldiers.

He's not prepared for the photos. Damn, the building's been sucked of its innards, room after ghost-like room. Cement shards litter the floors as though the place were undergoing a planned demolition, and the stairway walls are pocked, like they took bazooka hits from an assaulting army. Six stories tall, but it's a structure that might cave in on itself momentarily. God knows, it's a wonder any beams are standing. In the hollowed interior, metal desks have flown about, and woodwork pieces now poke up from rubble piles, while electrical wires hang like party streamers. Some party! Jesus, these people knew what they were doing!

One of the agents tells him that the blast broke windows in surrounding buildings, one of them a block away. An overhead aerial shot is being developed as they speak, but The Bureau hasn't seen destruction on this scale in all of the anti-war activity they've tracked.

"Professionals," he says knowingly to the briefing agents. "These aren't your everyday students. They've planned this for years."

Haven't they? For a second, in the thin morning light entering the windows, he wonders. *Who are they, these people?*

Harris Point, 1962-63 (Eight Years Earlier)

Years later, as a fugitive, James Brandes would see things differently, with a sharp sense of time and place having been stolen from him. Today he thought all experience was wonderfully his forever.

There were three of them. In a large field six blocks from James' home, they were playing at home plate, making the dust there into balls in their fists and then throwing the balls so that the dust powdered into a chalk-white veil against the blue sky.

The things they made were there, and then not, but they were magically changed in going.

Randy made the hardest dust clods and threw them the farthest. Randy always seemed to have to stand out above everyone. After Randy came himself, then Howard, who was fat, some of the neighborhood kids said. Howard was only pudgy, but he couldn't throw dustballs or baseballs well and always came in last in running. Sometimes when the three of them were riding their bikes, Randy would start a race, and James would lag back so that Howard came in second.

One day Randy caught him doing it and called him a chicken. They had a real race then, which Randy won, but just by half a wheel-length, and Randy never called him that again.

They'd been packing and throwing the dust balls for half an hour when Randy quit and wandered over to the rickety backstop screen behind home plate. "Who's climbing with me?" he shouted.

"Better not," Howard said, as Randy grabbed the wire webbing with his hands. Then he put his tennis shoe toes into the too-small holes, and spidered his way to the top. When he got there he swung one leg over the green two-by-four and sat there straddling it. "I'm a mountain climber, the only one who made it!" he crowed.

The backstop swayed dangerously with Randy's weight on top, and from below he thought he could hear one of the support pieces cracking.

"Watch it," he yelled up. "You'll hurt yourself. You'll break it."

"Who cares? I'm the man on the mountain top." Randy moved the backstop recklessly, shifting his weight so the supports made a wrenching noise, of rusty nails giving way.

By this time Howard, who'd grown frightened and didn't want to show it, had wandered over to the long grass near first base. There he'd found a huge, lame moth with grey-brown wings and bright green spots.

The spots reminded James of colors in a pair of his mother's metallic earrings. The markings were beautiful, the size of dimes and as shiny.

"He looks stunned," Howard said. "Is that his own dust on his wings?"

"I think so. Better not rub it off."

"What'll we do with him?"

"Lift him over into the weeds. Look at that thick black fur on his body. Wow!"

Over his shoulder, as they carried the moth toward a refuge, they heard Randy calling. "What is it?" He was still looking down on them.

"A moth. He's hurt."

"Kill it," Randy shouted, "it's weak!" He swung the backstop in rhythm with the words.

As they got close to the weeds, the moth stirred then suddenly burst with a powerful wing thrust out of Howard's hands into flight. It headed toward thick brush.

Howard was scared into a light-headed surprise, and James felt it too for a minute. Later, calmed, he thought how good it felt to save something.

His family, the Brandeses, lived in a city of thirty thousand people, on its eastern edge. Behind their house was farmland once, but now there were new homes in large tracts of land.

Every six months a new tract was being opened. Down in the heart of town were old stores abandoned at one time but now restored. On the south edge of town, near the lake and city park, a big new series of stores, called a mall, had been constructed.

His dad was on something called the Chamber of Commerce. Once when he was very young he actually tried to find the place, the chamber, in an alley off main street. Later he understood there wasn't any chamber or building at all; the people like his dad met in a room in the YMCA. He hoped no one would find out how stupid he was, and luckily no one did.

The year before, Harris Point won an award for Best Redeveloped Midwestern City, 1961, and his dad was very proud of the Chamber's work.

When he was younger, he walked to school, past the sporting goods store his family owned. Now he would walk to the corner at the end of his street where he would board the bus to Roosevelt Junior High School, where he was in the seventh grade.

On Sunday his mother got them up early enough so that they could take a bath, get dressed in pressed shirts and dresses, shine shoes, and have a big breakfast, all before going to church. If it was a special day, they would have something unusual for breakfast.

Today his father noticed the blueberry muffins before the rest of them did, smelling them from upstairs. "What's the occasion, Janine?" he asked, coming downstairs and sitting at the table.

"No special reason," his mother said, but her voice was airy.

"I bet it's the new minister, isn't it?" his father said. Today was the first time their new pastor was speaking as the head of the church. He'd been chosen at a meeting of the deacons a month before.

"Maybe." His mother radiated satisfaction.

"Maybe yes," his father grinned back, nudging James in the ribs with his elbow. "This family's never going to run out of religious feelings as long as your mother's around, eh, James? Wendy?"

She looked at them sternly, giving his father an extra harsh glance. Then she brightened: "Would you like to sit with your friends today, James, instead of with us? Twelve-year-old's should be allowed to do that."

"Sure. Thanks."

His father asked his mother if she didn't think the new pastor was a little young. Didn't he seem immature in some way?

"He's just boyish," she answered. "I like him immensely."

"But you only spent two minutes with him at the open house the other night."

"I just have a good feeling about him."

"And every other minister you've ever met." His father sneaked out a trace of amusement she didn't catch, which was what he hoped for.

That was the moment when Wendy spilled her orange juice and sent everyone else scurrying for sponges and used napkins. She got it on her dress and had to go wash it out, with her mother's help.

They were late getting to church and had to slip into one of the back pews. There was no time for him to go sit elsewhere with his friends.

The minister, leading the choir in a hymn, had a clear, strong voice.

During the sermon he talked about being a good Christian. It didn't mean just showing up for services on Sunday. If you were a Christian it meant being one all week long, treating people fairly, helping those less fortunate, and understanding that people were different from one another in ways that God had planned.

After service, outside, he heard his father talking to a friend. "Well, at least he didn't raise a lot of hell with us," his dad joked, looking around to see that he wasn't being heard by others. "Give him ten or twelve more Sundays, he'll find something to get after us about."

In the car on the way home his mother made Wendy report what she learned in Sunday School. Then she said Pastor Allen was a fine person. The congregation would like him.

That was his mother's nice side, and most of the time she was nice about everything. But one night he overheard a conversation that showed how she could get upset too. With the lights out in his room, with him supposedly asleep, he could hear his dad trying to calm his mother down.

"Look," he was saying, "every generation finds something to glom onto. You were ga-ga about Sinatra, I remember."

"I was never like these girls are, Ralph. Never!"

"You were, Janine, but you were prettier."

"Ralph, please." His mother was seeing through his dad's flattery.

"Well, you were. Still are. Don't worry, they'll get over rock and roll."

"But Wendy's only ten. I found an Elvis poster in her closet last week."

His dad tried a joke: "Did she get pregnant from it yet?"

"Stop it, Ralph. This is serious. These people want to tear things down, things we stand for. They're wild! Wild animals some of them!"

"It's only music, for heaven's sake."

His mother wouldn't give up: "Go ahead, laugh it away. The marijuana, too, that these people use. They've had no religious upbringing."

His dad sounded a little beaten: "Can I go to sleep now? I've got inventory to do tomorrow, lots of work."

"I'm getting up. Do you think Pastor Allen would know what to do? Should I call him?"

"He may have inventory to do, too, Janine, counting hymnals, maybe. Try some warm milk first." By the time he heard his mother downstairs in the kitchen, his father was snoring.

She was his sister, so he was supposed to like her, and he did, usually, but lately she and her friends were driving him crazy.

He would be reading in his room. Wendy and Josi and Pam would be in Wendy's room, next door, and they would start giggling. It would start slowly at first, something like a sneeze, from one of them. Then another would make the noise, and after a minute the third would be doing it. Then two or three would do it together for a while. After that all three of them would be doing it constantly, so that the whole upstairs would be full of ridiculous noise.

He couldn't read so he would shout to Wendy to be quiet, and she would say that they would be, but then it would start again, and he would bang on the wall and shut his door, but it was impossible to concentrate.

"Make them stop, please," he begged his mother, downstairs.

"It's just a phase they're going through. Why don't you go down to the family room?"

"But I like being in my own place upstairs."

"I know. And I appreciate how good you are to your sister."

"I'd just like her to stop that dumb noise."

"She's young," his mother said, "and you shouldn't have to put up with this, but sometimes we have to."

It made things easier for him if he remembered when Wendy was small, when the family called her Speedster because she always raced through the house.

The two of them made up a game they played. Wendy would race toward him, he'd act like he didn't see her coming, then at the last minute he'd bolt out his arm so that she'd be blocked or get knocked over in trying to pass him. If she got knocked over, he'd get to pick her up and tickle her to make her feel better, and tickle her more and hug her.

She learned how to get back at him, though. She'd race toward him, but she'd time herself so that she'd speed up before he raised his semaphore arm. Or she'd zoom into a split-second stop, do an about-face, and walk away from him, leaving him looking silly.

He was trying to understand how he had misspelled the word "vicious"on his test an hour before. It seemed so easy now that he looked at it.

He almost didn't hear Miss Cassidy when she called on him.

"James," she said, "what is the Mexican word for a house?" She was a large woman who loved travel south of the border. She'd been there twice during her summer vacations.

"Hacienda," he said.

"Very good. You're doing very well at this. Howard too."

He looked over at Howard four rows away, who was beaming as much as he ever did, in his gawky, shy way. He'd gotten that way from being teased too much by the other kids.

"Gene," Miss Cassidy went on, "what do the Mexicans eat? Right, Cindy: beans and rice. But raise your hand next time."

Then Miss Cassidy made an announcement. "Now," she said with excitement on her face, "I want to tell you that later we're going to learn a Mexican song. And we're going to sing it in Spanish. But let's go outside for recess first."

They all tore outside. On the way he heard one kid ask another what was so great about learning a Spanish song, so he was careful not to mention he liked the idea. Still, he thought it would be fun since he liked the sound of Spanish. "Hacienda" came on a breeze out of your chest. "Gaucho" came from somewhere deep near your stomach.

After recess they sang the Mexican song called "La Cucaracha," and when Miss Cassidy told them that meant a cockroach, everyone laughed. Randy, next to him, laughed the longest, and even when the rest of the class settled down, he was still smothering chortles. Miss Cassidy let him go on for a while, hoping he would stop by himself, but he kept it up.

"Randy!" she shot at him finally. Her voice cracked like a whip as she waved the rest of the class to a stop.

Randy drew himself up in his seat.

"Young man, you will stop that laughing or go to the principal!"

The class waited to see what move Randy would make. He didn't like being called down, and they knew it, and Miss Cassidy knew it.

He lowered one shoulder, glancing out of one corner of his eye toward his teacher. He set his lips and wrinkled his brows. He was going to sulk.

Miss Cassidy let him be that way five minutes then insisted he join in the singing. He tried to keep up but couldn't, which made her lose her patience again.

"Follow along!" she said sternly. "Show him, James."

He knew something about Randy that Miss Cassidy didn't know, but he was unsure of saying something. He finally decided to. "He can't read the notes. The week we learned that, he was out with pneumonia."

"I can too, read 'em!" Randy interrupted. He was getting mad again.

"I'll teach him during free period tomorrow," he put in quickly.

"Thank you, James. Class, let's go on."

Afterwards, as they were leaving school, Randy came up to him. "You aren't gonna to teach me nothing," he snarled.

"It's not hard to learn, you know—reading music."

"Why'd you tell on me?"

"I was helping you out. You shouldn't fake things."

Randy clammed up. "Maybe," he said, grudgingly, finally, as he walked off.

He had trouble understanding what made Randy tick, why he would fight learning something when it was fun to learn anything.

On TV that same night, before dinner, he watched some American soldiers moving about in a field. The first pictures were from a helicopter above them, and they looked like ants. Then there were pictures from the ground, showing the soldiers walking through weeds taller than themselves.

A reporter was using strange words: Veesee and Arvun.

A soldier speaking into a microphone talked about someone called Victor Charlie and said Kay-eye-hay.

Something like a scoreboard appeared on the screen, and then he could figure out some of the strangeness. Arvun meant A.R.V.N, Veesee meant V.C., and K.I.A. meant killed in action because it was next to a column with the heading "Wounded." He asked his father, who was reading the newspaper, to explain things for him.

"We're fighting a war in a place called Vietnam, James. We're against the communists, who are the Viet Cong. The ARVN's are our friends. They're in the south; the communists hold the northern part of the country."

"Is it a big war?"

"No, it should be over in a year or so."

They watched together for a minute longer. At the end of the report some soldiers were shown loading green plastic bags into the helicopter.

"Are those supplies, Dad?"

"No, son. They're bodies of dead soldiers."

"Enemy soldiers?"

"No, James, ours. Well not ours, really. Our troops are only advisors there, telling the South Vietnamese what to do."

His father went back to his reading, saying nothing else, and he recalled being at his dad's business, helping out one day a month before, when a man came in. After a while it became obvious that the man wanted to talk about something, about some decisions being made in Washington, tied to that same war, in Asia, on the TV tonight.

His dad kept saying things like "Could be that's true," and "Gee, I hadn't really thought about that," and "Thanks for telling me your opinions." He was being overly pleasant in strange ways and seemed eager to change the subject.

When the man left, having bought a new fishing rod, his dad came over to where he was sorting bass lures. "Let that be a lesson, James. That guy wanted to talk politics in the worst way, but I didn't let myself get drawn in. Good business and politics just don't mix."

He told his dad he didn't understand.

"It's simple, son. If you happen to disagree with them, they won't buy anything."

Now he felt like talking about the things in his mind, and about the man in the store and the green plastic body bags. If he didn't talk about it, he thought, he might be haunted by what he'd seen tonight. But he didn't have any idea about where to begin, so he just left the room. And he was haunted for months.

That summer he learned everything he could about meteorology and astronomy.

It all started a week or two after school let out for vacation, when he read an article about tornadoes. He got interested and checked out books from the library explaining rain, winds, relative humidity and barometric pressure, and low and high pressure areas.

He bought a barometer and thermometer, which he put up outside his bedroom window. He wrote away for weather maps from government agencies, and he would try to diagram frontal systems passing through the area. He got good enough to predict storms. Once, his forecast was more accurate than the one on TV.

One day toward the middle of summer he saw a magazine ad for a telescope kit he could build. He could use it to observe clouds, he thought, but later it turned out he used it more for looking at stars.

When he was making the telescope, he was not sure it would work, but the first night he set it up in the backyard, he caught the moon right off. It filled the whole lens, and he had the feeling he could reach out with his right hand and touch it. Its light was so intense it seemed white instead of yellow. He could spot the largest craters.

By summer's end he had taught himself where the major constellations and planets were. He could align them with each other by picking out key stars.

He brought Wendy to the back yard to show her, sneaking her out of the house after bedtime.

During the day, when he and Howard had nothing to do, he would ask Howard to test him on what he knew. He made a pack of note cards with questions on one side and answers on the other.

Howard would stumble through the difficult names: "What's the constellation between Ce-phe—?"

"Cepheus!"

"Cepheus and An–?, An-dro–?" His friend blushed at not getting the pronunciation right.

"Andromeda. That's Cassiopeia between them."

"Right. Where is–? How do you learn this stuff so easily, James?"

"I just do. You could too, if you wanted to."

"Not like you. You're so lucky smart, and I'm so, well, you know…." His friend was looking helpless for an instant, and he almost didn't know how to respond.

"You aren't. Don't tell yourself that."

"Okay. If you say so." The hesitancy hung on though: "Randy or Josh, they'd learn this stuff fast too, wouldn't they?"

"You're not Randy or Josh, How," he said. "You can't be them, but they can't be you either. That's the important thing."

Sometimes his dad would bring home new tackle he said the two of them needed to test. But his mother was on to them: "Just go fishing if that's what you want to do," she'd josh them. "Take Wendy this time. She might like it."

"Next time, Janine," his father would always say.

Today, though, Wendy had actually come along, out to Potter's Lake with them in the early morning.

His dad and he had made a secret pact not to put bait on Wendy's hook. "Let her squirm like the worm," his dad laughed. But then she surprised them by having no fear about what she was doing, diving right into the nightcrawlers and threading them onto her rig.

They cheered her on when she caught her first fish, a ten inch perch. In her excitement she rotated the reel the wrong way at first, so the perch might have gotten away, but it was well hooked. She reversed and got it to shore.

"It's a lunker, Janine!" his dad yelled, leading them into the house an hour later. He pulled his daughter out from behind him: "Wendy, bring that log of a fish here for your mother to see!" Later, he had great fun making a grand do of her success, finding the camera in the desk drawer, having her pose in the driveway with a fishing rod and a funny hat on.

The mood carried through the whole afternoon to right before dinner, when he was reading the paper at the kitchen table, letting his enthusiasm light in another place: "Looks like we're finally getting smart over there, Janine?"

"Where? Who?" She looked up only briefly from the casserole she was preparing.

"Sorry. Vietnam. We're sending actual troops there now, to fight."

"But nobody's attacked us, Ralph. It's not like Pearl Harbor."

"It will be if we let it get out of hand. It's like dominoes, the Pentagon's saying. First one country goes, then another, and then another. Kind of a neat way to look at the whole thing, don't you think?"

His mother seemed on the verge of saying something but then held back.

"C'mon, out with it, Janine," his dad prodded. His face suddenly had mystification all over it.

"No, I'll make you angry."

"How so? Did you hear me, what I said just now?"

His mother looked ready to respond, but then she changed the subject: "I need you to take out the garbage," she said, turning her back.

His dad took his grudging sweet time getting up, heading for the waste can. "Don't tell me later that I didn't give you a chance to speak your mind," he muttered.

After dinner, when his father was downstairs in his workshop, he asked his mom what she was going to say earlier. Even then she seemed reluctant, but she finally relented. "All this war business," she said, "it's like a game or something, to men. Countries like dominoes! But it's not a game once the bodies start coming home, is it?"

"I guess not," he started to say, when she cut him off, a thing she almost never did.

"And here I've probably gotten angry at you because you're going to be one of those men, too, one day. I knew I shouldn't have said anything."

"I pushed you to tell me," he said. "It's my fault."

"Maybe you'll be different." The words came with crippled conviction though.

The week before school started they were out playing kick-the-can, after dark at Howard's house, Justin Zimmerman, Josh Seybold, and Howard and himself.

During a break in the game, down the street came Randy and Dan Norman.

"Want to join in?" Josh asked.

"Naw, we're into some real fun. Right, Dan?" Randy's usual swagger stance was outlined in the streetlight's white sphere.

"Like what?" Howard asked.

"You'll have to come with, to see," Randy said.

Randy and Dan led them along three blocks toward a construction site. Before they got to it, though, Randy took them behind some bushes about forty yards from the house being built.

"We're doing a window a night," he said smugly.

"What do you mean?" Josh spoke for the rest of them.

"You just take this sling shot," Randy said, "and you take a rock and—" He bent down to pick up something from the ground.

"We got the bedroom window last night," Dan bragged, as Randy let the rock whip away from him. They heard the sound of it hitting the house's plywood sheeting.

"It's perfect," Randy said. "There's nobody around to hear a thing. We could do this all night."

"But—" Josh and he spoke at the same time.

"What's the problem, James?"

"You could get arrested for this."

"We take turns." Randy was handing the sling-shot to Dan.

"I'm leaving," he said, thinking of what his folks would feel about him being in a situation like this. "This is dangerous."

"Me too," Josh and Howard chimed in.

"Maybe I'll come along. It's late." Dan seemed uneasy all of sudden.

"No guts," Randy laughed. "See ya."

But as soon as they left, they saw Randy coming after them, a half block behind.

Everybody—Randy, him, Howard, Josh, Dan and David Norman—was growing so fast, it seemed like they were born to bump into things all the time. His legs and arms didn't coordinate like they used to. Clothes he'd worn the previous year looked like they were part of a Halloween costume, and he couldn't wear a favorite jacket now, one he'd almost lived in the last two years.

He felt unsure of himself a lot of times, as though he and Howard had traded personalities.

Sometimes he was terribly embarrassed at things his parents did, when he knew he shouldn't be. When his family went out to dinner, his father would stack up the plates for the waitress at the end of the meal, if she were busy. He tried to hide his cringing over his father's helpfulness.

He felt sorry for Howard, who thought he'd lose some of his fleshy look when he grew taller. His friend didn't look much thinner with his added height.

As for Randy, he was swearing a lot now, especially around girls, who would be shocked and skate away from his crude talk. But minutes later they'd be back talking to him eagerly, as though they liked him for his wild words. He could talk to girls better than any of the guys.

At home James tried out some of the swear words himself, forming the syllables in front of the mirror and half-tumbling, half-talking the sounds out of his mouth. He just sounded silly trying to be something he wasn't. He could manage "damn" pretty well, but whenever he went beyond that, he just had to give up.

The woman TV reporter in Saigon was saying that Madame Nhu was as chic as Jackie Kennedy. She'd been raised in French schools when the French occupied Vietnam. She spoke English and French fluently, made frequent trips to Europe, and gave social life in the country a great deal of style.

"She's certainly striking," his mother said. She'd just come into the living room, having finished the last tidying-up of the kitchen.

"No question about that!" his dad chimed in, as the camera focused and swept through a huge hall with crystal chandeliers.

Waiters in stiff white shirts were moving among the crowd, holding trays on their shoulders. At the center of the crowd the woman called Madame Nhu was wearing an expensive dress that fit her thin, angular body perfectly. Makeup on her high cheekbones caught the lights from above her. People around her were pushing away others to talk to her.

The reporter said that Madame Nhu had confided something important, that a Paris designer had made her dress, for a thousand dollars.

"You want one like that, Janine?" his dad whistled. "Maybe if I had a special sale on duck decoys, we could set you up in something like that."

His mother was about to say that she'd settle for a new purse, when the camera flashed to the outside of the presidential palace, at a different time. Stepping out of a limousine was Madame Nhu's brother-in-law, the president of the country, Mr. Diem.

The reporter's voice went on: "While Madame Nhu represents something to aspire to, she also represents a class of people Vietnam's peasants and shopkeepers resent. Unlike Jackie Kennedy, she is seen as arrogant. There's also the question of how the Nhus and Diems acquired their large fortune. They have never owned any business."

His mother fumed a moment: "You mean we bought that dress for her, our government? Our taxes?"

"It's only a dress, hon," his father answered. "Don't worry your pretty head about it."

When his dad said that, he missed something the reporter ended with. James thought it was a comment that the South Vietnamese government was less and less popular with the people.

On the way to the lake next morning he asked his father why they were going at this time of year. Usually, early September was past the time when they would catch much. "Yeah, but fishing's good any time," his dad answered, "like my best customers say." He didn't seem concerned about their prospects, for some reason.

In the cool air they fished for an hour and caught only a single bluegill. Standing twenty yards down the bank from his father, he couldn't understand why his elder was whistling happily. Most of the time when they weren't catching fish, his dad became restless and impatient.

"Hey, James?"

"What?"

"There's an oblong box in the trunk. Want to get it for me?"

"Sure. What's in it?"

"A surprise."

When he brought the box back, his father opened it eagerly.

"I thought I'd teach you how to shoot today," he said, as he lifted the small pistol from its case.

"Does Mom know about this?"

His dad's voice didn't miss a beat. "This is between you and me. Here, get the feel of it first. The safety's on."

He didn't really feel eager to take the gun. He was still haunted by the image on television of men with guns and men dead in combat. He knew he shouldn't be making such connections, but he couldn't stop them from going through his thoughts, and once he'd gotten a headache from thinking about all of it.

"It's okay," his dad said, sensing his nervousness. "It takes a little getting used to."

They walked to a nearby area, a gravel pit, where his dad set up a tin can on a log. Meanwhile he was still holding the twenty-two awkwardly, so his dad took it back.

"This is the right stance," his dad said, firing a shot. The sound was sharper than he thought, though he knew it would be loud, and he winced, not wanting to.

"Now you try, without shells first. Unless you don't want to."

"Huh uh, I want to," he lied, taking the weapon. Inside, his chest felt tight, and it seemed like there was a small, wild bird loose somewhere under his shirt.

He had toy pistols as a boy, but when he pulled the trigger on those, the parts didn't work together well, so you had to really yank your finger. On this gun you barely applied any pressure to make the mechanical parts go click, a click too smooth.

"Good. Let me load it for you. I'm giving it to you with the safety on. Release that after you take your stance."

"Easy now," his father went on. "Just squeeze off on it."

When the gun went off, it seemed like his hand went out of control, no longer his own. His arm wanted to salute, and yet his wrist swivelled like it had no bone. The thing in his hand felt alive.

"That's it," his father said. "Now this time don't jerk the trigger so much."

But when he held the gun up again, his hand was shaking, and he didn't squeeze but pulled the trigger hard. A full six yards from the target, brush disintegrated as the steel thing in his hand just went crazy. A third shot went off, into the air. As the sounds died down, he could feel his father's large hand on top of his on the gun, and he could hear the words "Maybe we'll try this some other time."

They fished for an hour more. Once or twice he spotted his father looking at him, trying to smile but showing disappointment he couldn't hide.

On the way home he could tell his father's mood from the way the car slowed and sped up erratically. Normally, his father's speed never wavered on the open stretches.

He felt bad, embarrassed all over, as they turned into the driveway. Not looking his father in the face, he said: "I'm sorry about the shooting."

His father tried to shrug off what had happened: "That's a really good bluegill you got," he said, into the dashboard.

A week later, on a Saturday morning, he was finally stirring at 11:30. In the warmth of the covers and under his mauled pillow, he'd just been reliving times when he was younger, six or seven years old, he thought.

His dad would sneak into his bedroom at times on mornings like this. He'd wake him up by whispering nonsense things in his ear. "Two and two minus six is ten," he'd say. "Jack and Jill went up the hill to catch a pail of...Cheerios!" And "You're the famous baseball player with a violin. Your name is Stan Musical."

He was growing up, but he knew he'd always remember the moments.

Today he just wanted to sleep longer. He'd been up till two, when his mother found him with his light still on. He knew it bothered her, his staying up till all hours, but he just couldn't break his weekend habits. One time he was up till four, finishing a book, giving in to that strange power all books had over him. He could read and read and read, and then go back and read again.

When he finally got downstairs, at noon, he found his mother repainting the kitchen. Usually neat in appearance and well-groomed, she still loved putting her hair up in a bandanna, donning old slacks, and going after scarred walls with a fresh coat of whatever color was fashionable. Today she was applying a pale salmon.

"Hi, Mom," he said. "Looks like we're eating out tonight, 'ey?"

"What do you think of the color? Not too intense?"

"It's fine, but we'll need new curtains."

"I already picked them out," she said proudly. "They're in the living room."

He watched her do the edges, working quickly, singing or humming as she went along, and he felt glad for her.

A drop of paint fell on the newspaper on the floor, on the edge of a photo, and the photo itself brought him out of his last waking sluggishness. A memory, one struggling for notice among those he had earlier, jumped into his mind, making him flinch a little.

The photo was of a Buddhist priest burning himself to death in the streets of Saigon, the capitol of South Vietnam.

They'd seen the actual event on TV right before dinner, as they went to the table, and they were horrified at what they saw. Calmly, without any fear, the priest let himself be doused in gasoline. Then the fire began, and he sat in a strangely rigid but untroubled state. As he died, his body leaned a bit, the flames charring his clothing and finally his skin.

His mother was so shaken at the time, she'd tried to shield Wendy from watching. She hurried her daughter into the kitchen.

They hadn't talked about what they'd seen, until the end of the meal, when he asked his dad why the priest did the awful thing.

"I dunno, James. He was probably a communist in disguise, working against what we're trying to accomplish over there."

"But the reporters said that wasn't the case at all." His mother seemed drawn in, despite her inclinations to let the matter end. "The government doesn't want them practicing their religion."

"The reporters don't know what they're talking about. I've told you that." His dad's impatience with his mother seemed almost like a reflex, and his tone was almost mean for a second or two.

"But if it's true—people can't worship as they want—well, why are we there?"

His dad pushed his plate away, his meal finished, his voice softer: "Well it sure proves what we learned in the war and Korea, about those Asians not caring about life as deeply as we do."

"We talked about that in school once," he said to his dad, nervous about challenging him. "My teacher said that only a few Japanese were willing to kill themselves. At the end of the war, when we were going to invade Japan."

"Not true, James. You take any Oriental, they just don't hold life as important as we do."

Wendy interrupted: "You mean Mama Su's going to set herself on fire too, in front of her laundry? Right on Fifteenth Street?"

His mom and dad both laughed at Wendy, thinking she was joking, but he saw that she was frightened. Her foot was twirling madly beneath the table, and he wanted to comfort her, but he didn't know how because she was separated from him.

Luckily, they finally understood too, his mother before his dad.

"She's probably the exception, Sugar," his dad said, comfortingly. After Wendy got over her embarrassment, he drawled out, "A little burning like that would sure tie up traffic mid-town." He laughed again, a little nervously this time, eyeing Wendy for reactions.

"That's what everybody at bridge club was asking today," his mother said a week later as the waitress finishing pouring water into their glasses. "What's that Madame Nhu going to do for fancy dresses now that her brother-in-law and husband are out of power?"

"A little more than out of power," his dad chuckled. "Riddled with bullets is about as out of power as you can get."

"Oh, I know. What I meant was–! Well, you know."

They were out to dinner at the small family restaurant they went to about once a week, and Wendy was bugging him, kicking his shin under the table. He was having trouble following the conversation, so after the waitress left, he asked his dad to explain.

"There's a new government in Vietnam," his dad said. "Some new people took over yesterday. They shot the old president and his brother."

"Wow! Pretty serious, huh?"

"It's all for the best," his dad reassured him. "At least that's what Washington thinks."

Hearing his father say that, he felt better about what he'd heard. Ralph Brandes was practically always right about things, people in the community said.

His dad really loved his mom, too. Most of the time he just did his business and read his newspaper when he got home, but once he did something that showed how much he cared. He took some money he'd been saving up and tried to make her buy a dress with it. It was when James was about ten years old.

"But I've got a perfectly good dress for nice occasions," his mom was saying, down in the new rec room they'd created from the unfinished basement.

"That's not the point, Janine," his father was telling his mother. "You deserve to go down to that new mall place and splurge. Buy a new coat if you don't want another dress."

"It's so extravagant though."

"Our families watched pennies when we were growing up. We don't have to be like that."

"You're sure about this?" Being the one who kept the accounting books for the store, she couldn't understand that her Ralph had kept a special fund for this occasion, for her. And she wanted to be happy but didn't quite know how.

As he left off eavesdropping in the upstairs hallway, he could hear his mother finally saying how nice it was to not worry about finances. Maybe she'd buy a dress for herself and one for Wendy. She'd have to figure out how to do something nice for her son too.

His teachers were acting strange. Mr. Rollins, the vice-principal, stopped at the door of their English class to tell Mrs. Hart something. Then five minutes later Mrs. Hart told them to study by themselves for a while, and she left the room. Then Mrs. Hart came back, and right after that Mr. Humphries, who taught woodworking, stuck his head in the door and told Mrs. Hart something. All of the teachers seemed to be talking very seriously.

"What's up?" Howard said to him. He said it too loudly, and he looked like he expected the two of them to be called down for his volume, but Mrs. Hart just looked at them as though she didn't care. She looked scared herself in a way.

Later Mr. Humphries came back to talk with Mrs. Hart, who seemed to shake a little when talked to. She nodded and went to her desk after Mr. Humphries left a second time. She drew a paper tissue from a drawer, and he thought he caught her dabbing at something in her eye.

She stood up, heavily for a thin woman, and told them. President Kennedy had been shot a half hour before. Now he was dead.

She told them there would be no more studying that hour, that they could sit quietly and talk if they wanted.

Two of the girls in the class started crying, and Mrs. Hart said that was perfectly natural to do that. No one should feel ashamed of their feelings.

One of the boys asked if he could go to his locker and get a transistor radio he had there. Mrs. Hart said that would be a good idea, that maybe they might feel better if they knew some more information.

When the boy got back to class, everyone tried to listen, but the radio's batteries were weak. A boy and two girls in the back row said they felt a little sick. Were people trying to kill other government officials and take over the country?

Mrs. Hart said she didn't think so. The country was strong.

There would be a large funeral for the president, she thought, and probably there would be no school the following Monday.

He asked Howard if he'd ever been to a funeral. He'd never been to one himself.

Howard said he hadn't either. "Will we be scared?" he asked back.

"We'll all be together at least, How."

At home they watched television for almost three full days. On the first day they saw films of the assassination in Dallas: the president's car in a line of cars, pulling out and racing to the hospital, then the scene at the hospital, and later the president's body being loaded onto a plane headed for Washington, where that Mister Johnson was being sworn into office. A man named Lee Harvey Oswald had been arrested for killing Kennedy and was being held in the Dallas jail, but nobody was sure he had done it. Everything seemed confusing.

On the second day there were ceremonies in Washington, where people gave speeches called eulogies in places called rotundas. Senators and other important people were identified by the news cameras as the cameras surveyed the crowds.

That night the casket with the president's body in it was placed in a small, domed building. Military guards stood by it, and thousands of people filed by it all night long, people with baffled and shocked looks. It was impossible not to be sad, and he cried once that night, quietly into his pillow, in his room after he went to bed.

On Sunday afternoon the man named Oswald was shot in the Dallas jail and died too. He was being taken from one section of the jail to another, when a man with a revolver stepped out from a group of detectives and shot him in the stomach.

It happened right on television. He and millions of people saw the killing as it happened, with Oswald trying to put his hand in front of himself, too late, to catch the bullet so it wouldn't go inside of him. His whole face looked horribly drawn out of shape as he felt the bullet tearing up things inside him.

The third day started with a mass in a church. Then the funeral procession made its way toward Arlington National Cemetery, where the President was to be buried. Mrs. Kennedy, her children, and the members of the Kennedy family stood among the important people. Mrs. Kennedy was dressed in black, a color people wore when someone close to them died, his mother said.

The president's body was carried on something called a caisson, a platform pulled by horses. Behind it a lone soldier walked, holding a single white horse, with a black saddle whose stirrups were tied to the top of the saddle so that no one could have ridden. His mother told him and Wendy that the riderless horse was a symbol of a fallen commander-in-chief.

Leaders from foreign countries marched behind the First Lady. Bands played long, slow hymns. Drummers drummed a steady, slow-walking beat. Along the procession route flags flew at half staff.

At Arlington National Cemetery the last ceremony was held in a small, square area surrounded by a simple, white picket fence. A priest said a short prayer, then someone lighted a torch held on a short, slender pole. The television newscaster said that the torch would always be kept lighted, as an eternal flame, a sign to all mankind of the goodness the president did for the world's people. That goodness would never be taken away.

"Will we ever have anything happen to us like this again?" he asked his parents.

"Probably not, James," his father tried to reassure him. "That Oswald, he was sick, see. There aren't many of those around that the FBI doesn't know about."

"I wish I had your confidence, Ralph," his mother countered. "I just don't know, with all this crime around nowadays. I pray a lot about that."

He thought it was a good time to ask his mother a question that had been troubling him since the killing was announced in his English class four days before. "Mom, if God is good, then why did he let this awful thing happen?"

His mother had to take minute before she answered. "Do you remember the Book of Job, James?"

"That's where all those terrible things happen to that simple man?"

"Yes. Well, sometimes God has to test our faith, to make us endure things as proof. It's hard to understand, isn't it?"

"Yes."

"That's the point. Some things we can't understand, and we just have to accept. Does that make sense?"

"Yes." But it didn't make sense, as hard as he tried to figure it out in the weeks ahead. He kept thinking about guns and shooting and far-away places where people lifted green plastic body bags into helicopters. Would it all stop sometime?

Harris Point, Fall 1965—Summer 1966

On the run decades later, blending into places, hiding his face and learning the art of being inconspicuous, he would say to himself: *At least you had that one time, the years when you were someone, James. More than that, people like you cared for each other—family, friends, neighbors, acquaintances on your city's streets. People took pride in their care, and there was not this jackal-like thing from Washington ready to roam Harris Point's streets and tear apart its way of life. But the thing was at the city's edge, waiting, eyeing it. You should have seen that.*

He was older and everything was more complicated now, but he felt more confidence in himself, these first few months of his junior year in high school.

This late September afternoon, passing through the living room before dinner, he was about to ask his dad if he could mow the lawn next day instead of today. But he waited since his dad seemed caught by something in the news.

A commentator was saying that the government the U.S. was supporting in South Vietnam really wasn't a government as we ordinarily thought of it. It was a family in control but not much control since it had never been chosen in a popular elections.

His dad seemed to be carrying on an argument with the face on the TV screen. "Better than the damn commies!" He was pointing at the set, scolding it.

He asked his dad if the war was going badly.

Only in the eyes of reporters, his dad replied, with a grumpiness he rarely showed. He added that was often the case. Wars took time to win, like in Korea where a breakthrough in the fighting took a long time coming. Soldiers had to be patient, and so did people back home. They had to have faith in their leaders.

He'd always wondered about his dad's service in Korea, expecting him to tell stories of being in combat, but his dad said now that he'd only served in a supply company, in the rear areas, like most troops in most wars. The winters in Korea were brutally cold with inadequate gas heaters barely warming tents and supply warehouses. Engines and mechanisms wouldn't work because even grease froze.

It was frustrating for him not to be able to fight the enemy directly those days, and he hoped coming generations of Brandeses would get to be in the thick of things when it came time for them to serve.

Leaving the room, his dad's attention back on the TV program, for the first time it occurred to him that if the present war went on, he might have to be the next-generation soldier his dad was referring to. But his dad seemed assured the conflict would end soon.

Upstairs in his room he tried to think of how he might act in battle, and he remembered the day a couple of years before, out fishing, when his father tried to teach him how to shoot. He couldn't convey to his dad —he didn't even realize it at the time—how the idea of guns, any guns, bothered him. Then Kennedy had been killed with a gun, and now guns were killing people in the big cities.

Months after that day at the lake, he heard another conversation he shouldn't have heard, between his parents.

"He's sensitive, Ralph," his mother was saying. "He's different than you. If he wants to learn to shoot, he'll let you know."

"A guy should know how to handle a weapon." His dad's tone boomed with gruff assertion.

"He'll come to you," his mother said. "Let him decide when."

"*When* might be *never* is the problem."

He thought now that he should think about trying to learn to shoot since he didn't want to disappoint his parent. But he really hated it. No, he wouldn't do it, he decided. Couldn't if he even wanted to, since he didn't have the heart for it.

His days were happy now because of Heather, Heather Dickinson from his junior-level Plane Geometry class, with a very definite favorite color. Behind her in the lunch line one day, he'd gotten to know her by asking why she wore red so much and had red notebooks and a red school bag.

"A bunch of reasons, which I'll tell you later," she teased him.

"Not now?"

"Now I have a crucial decision to make about a salad. You're James, right? Not Jim but James?"

"And you're Heather. Hi." He noticed two of her girl friends, at a nearby table, gossiping about them. He didn't care, nor did she, he could tell.

They went along the line picking out food and talking about their test the following day. He found out she hated asparagus and told her he'd remember that. She wanted to know what weird thing she should remember about him.

"I'll have to tell you later. I have this crucial decision to make now between a hamburger and a chili dog."

One day the following week he was in the library, trying to find a book, and when he returned to his study area, he found a note there, in his geometry text.

Why I Wear Reds

1. *Because I don't like green.*
2. *Because yellow disgusts me.*
3. *Because I saw a spy show on TV once where a beautiful woman who stole diamonds wore a red dress.*
4. *Because I like raspberries and strawberries which are colored ____________ (fill in the blank).*
5. *Because a person's entitled to a favorite color.*
6. *Because I am secretly a communist!!!*

When he looked up, laughing, he saw her outside the library, in the hall, grinning and waving. He grinned back as she left.

At the football game the following Saturday, he saw her in the stands and went to sit next to her. She had a big family, she told him, played the piano but was on the verge of giving it up, and adored her dog Coco. Her favorite thing was being with people, and she couldn't understand how he would hole up reading all the time. Did he really have five books checked out now, on architecture, when he didn't have to read any of them for a class?

Maybe he'd design a skyscraper some day, he said. He had to start learning early for something that big.

What would be neater, she suggested, was a new high school in Harris Point, one with mirrors, this time, in the girls' restrooms. The school board must have thought she and her friends wanted to be nuns.

He walked her home to her house, though it took him a mile out of his way, and decided he liked her. She wasn't part of a crowd in the school that was considered good-looking, but she was fun and genuine, and as he made his way home he kicked the dried leaves playfully.

Before bed he picked up one of the college catalogues he'd sent away for, which had been arriving almost every day now.

He wouldn't have any problems getting into most of the schools, he knew, and he could probably count on scholarships since his grade-point was good. In fact he was probably going to graduate in the top fifth of his class if he studied well in his last three semesters.

What he'd major in, he had no idea, and he knew he wouldn't have to decide for a very long time. Still, he thought it might be architecture. But then he was really interested in government, fascinated about how the U.S. had been formed and how the country struggled through the Civil War. He liked the idea of a balance of power between the branches of government, such a common-sense notion.

His mother said he shouldn't limit his choices of schools, that they had money for him and eventually Wendy. His dad said it wouldn't be a bad idea for him to go to the state university, since it would be cheaper there. Majoring in business would be good training for his being a partner in Brandes Sporting Goods, and maybe the two of them would open a second store.

Wendy stepped in for him that time, breaking the news: Her brother was more interested in making buildings than selling fishing poles and baseball bats. When their father seemed hurt, she punched him in the ribs as she sometimes did. "Don't worry, Pops. If he doesn't get into the business, I will." Then she bolted from the table to listen to her new Rolling Stones album for the fourth time that day.

Wendy and he had a little ritual about the Stones, and about music in general.

He loved Dylan and sometimes The Who. She loved The Stones like they were gods.

When they passed each other in the house, they would catch each other off guard by announcing their loyalties when the other one was preoccupied with something else.

"Dylan!" he'd say, as she went past him, her arms full of laundry.

"Mick!" she'd come back at him, if she were quick enough.

They had friendly arguments about their allegiances. He told her Mick Jagger was just a pair of big lips; you could stick him to the wall with them. She told him Dylan was a country hick.

The ritual went to another level when they developed a variation, waiting until the last second to do their zinger announcements, usually when one of them was leaving the house or a room. That way the other person couldn't answer back at all.

"The Stones!" she'd say.

"The Wh–!" he'd try to say back, but he'd be talking to the back door, which was banging shut as she scooted down the driveway.

He smiled when he thought of how fast she was at dominating the game. He liked her to win, and he thought that when they got older, at holiday times when they came back home, they'd probably take up the game again, as silly, nostalgic adults.

His mother had once talked about forbidding Wendy and him to have anything to do with the new rock music, but she gave up because the music was everywhere.

One night that fall they were even on TV, that rock music group the Beatles. Girls who were Wendy's age were at the edge of the stage, shrieking and jumping up and down. One had fainted, yelling "Paul! Paul!" The crowd pushing toward the stage was causing the camera to jiggle. The Beatles were barely able to hear, so when they played, the song came out jagged and uneven. They were laughing at the crowd but taken with it at the same time, surprised they were causing such a reaction.

His mother was in the kitchen, refusing to look at the program.

Wendy was right in front of the TV, her face almost pressed onto the screen.

"Hey, we can't see," his dad said. From the couch they were laughing at both Wendy and the TV audience.

"Pudlians?" his dad said. "What kind of word is that?"

"That's what they call people from Liverpool, Pop."

"Pretty crazy. Maybe your mother's right about all this stuff." But his dad's side-of-the-mouth amusement showed he didn't believe what he was saying.

If his mother was bothered by Wendy's music, she made up for it by her pleasure in going through college catalogs with him, trying to help choose a school. They would spread them out on the kitchen table, and she would spend hours with him, comparing various programs each school offered.

She and her father were glad for him, she said at the end of one of their evenings, even if his dad didn't show it much. Their generation hadn't had his opportunity.

"You'd have done well in college, Mom. I can picture you on a campus someplace."

"Now what makes you say that? I probably would have been frightened to death."

"Only for a little while. You know that."

"I suppose I would have," she admitted, a lark-light expression on her face for a second. "You're right."

She reached over and gave his hand a squeeze then drew back quickly. "Oops, I'm sorry," she said. "You're too old for that now, aren't you?"

"A little bit," he answered, squeezing back.

His dad was happy these days too, but not in the usual way, which he found out one night when he and Wendy met downstairs, jostling each other for position in front of the refrigerator. She asked him what he thought about their dad's idea for a little celebration, and he told her he didn't have any idea what she was talking about.

"That news story," Wendy explained, grabbing a soft-drink. "The president's sending a lot more troops to Asia, to end the war early."

"God, that war again. What's that got to do with the folks?"

"Dad said the two of them should go out to celebrate Johnson's decision. Like it was some birthday party event or something. Pretty strange, huh?"

"Strange is right."

"Mom didn't know how to react. She likes going out for dinner, but this—? She always thinks the worst, like the war will go on, and you'll have to be in it. But she doesn't want to hurt Pop's feelings."

"Dad says the war's going well now."

"He knows, I guess. I hope so, for your sake."

"Thanks."

Upstairs in his room, he again found himself having to think about his possibly going into the army sometime. He'd gotten to the point of knowing that it was something guys might have to do and even be proud of, but the war everybody was talking about just didn't seem like other wars the country had gotten into. He hated the confusion in his mind about what might happen.

The other, the Kennedy assassination insanity, weighed on him, too, like the first heavy snow on the lawn below him tonight. More than three years had gone by, but there was always a book, magazine or a news story saying that Kennedy had been shot by someone other than Oswald, or that Oswald hadn't acted alone, or that a group of people had planned the assassination.

He knew the speculation came from people who played on public fear, but it was almost impossible not to believe that in some way someone in the government had overlooked or deliberately hidden some vital fact.

He and Howard had similar moments when they felt taken in by the stupid theories. Howard said he had regular dreams about a group of men, probably in Washington but maybe elsewhere. They were in a barely lit room, seated around a finely polished table, in identical business suits. The words *Kennedy* and *Oswald* would be part of whispered discussions they were having, yet there would never be enough of their sentences to find out what the men were saying.

Wasn't it ridiculous, Howard said, that they both knew how irrational their thoughts were, but they kept having them anyway.

"Yeah, and I caught myself reading one of those hysteria articles in the supermarket checkout lane the other day. Thank god, nobody saw me."

While his dad seemed to have put fresh bounce in his walk, his mother, whom he'd always thought of as young and energetic, seemed to sigh a lot these winter days after Christmas. Wendy and he both noticed, and it was Wendy who tried to get her mother to talk, when the three of them were cleaning up after dinner one night.

"Is it so obvious?" her mother asked. "My mood? I'm sorry. I'll get over this."

"Mom, what's the *this* exactly?" He took a stack of saucers from her.

"I wish I could tell you, but I don't quite know. Isn't that silly?"

She handed Wendy a plate of food to scrape into the garbage, and her two offspring looked to each other, waiting for the other to go on, but neither knew where to begin again.

"A lot of it is this assassination talk, everyone still looking for some angle. It just wears me out. That poor woman, she deserves some peace, and no one will let her have it, after three years."

"But she's strong, don't you think?" he said. "I mean, I get bothered by this stuff too, but Mrs. Kennedy seems okay."

"Grief goes deep, James. It's worse with uncertainty mixed in."

Another silence settled on them, broken only by the sound of dishes and silverware going from clink to clack.

"The other—well, it's hard to explain. The crime of course. But all these other things, too, the drugs, black people demonstrating all over, the wild music!"

"Mom!"

"I know you don't want to hear this complaint all the time, Wendy, but—well, all of it, what I mentioned.... See, I can't just put it into words!" She tossed down a dishrag in frustration.

"Take your time, Mom," he told her.

"I just worry for you two. Things aren't like they used to be. Nothing's stable or predictable. Everything's different now."

Wendy tried some soothing: "We'll be okay, Mom."

"Will you?" His mother's face looked drawn, her thoughts roaming in some place in her head, remote from them." I hope so, dear God."

In Algebra class, at the start of the new semester, he and Randy watched Howard sending covert glances toward the new girl, Jennifer Sims. Their friend was trying hard to hide his interest, but it was clear he was infatuated. Howard also hadn't the slightest idea how to act on his feelings and was stewing himself into a desperate state of first love.

In the hallway after class, he saw Randy come up to Howard at his locker and tell him to borrow Jennifer's notes. Howard, trying to act innocent, said he had good ones, but Randy wouldn't let him duck the point: This was a convenient way to introduce himself.

His friend looked around nervously, hoping that no one was hearing their conversation, and Randy prodded on, lowering his voice to accommodate hapless Howard.

How was licking his lips rapidly now. "But I'm—" He made a gesture outlining the girth of his mid-section.

"And she's a little plain. God, just make your move! She knows you're going to, sooner or later."

"Really?"

Randy, astounded at Howard's innocence, bonked his head with his fist in mock disbelief as he wandered off to his next class, Howard having gone to his. Looking on, James couldn't help tapping his own head either.

Three days later, in the halls again, Howard was as happy as he'd ever seen him, gingerly holding Jennifer's notebook, as though it were platinum, and saying "Look, James!"

They waited a minute, until he left, before they gave into full laughter. "I'm in love, I'm all shook up!" Randy sang, doing an Elvis imitation with his hips, a routine he was known for around school.

Randy could be funny like that, but he could also show a streak that made you want to have nothing to do with him. Like that time when he'd been seeing Heather for about a month. His so-called friend came up to him one day in the hall as Heather was just strolling off to class, her back to them. Randy was closer than normal to him, saying in his ear: "You gettin' any of that?"

He'd backed away, as though Randy hadn't showered for weeks, hoping he wouldn't have to say anything else, the message being obvious. But Randy just kept up: "Whew, it's been a month now, James. Be a shame if you weren't scoring."

"It's none of your business!" he blurted after a moment, his anger obvious. *God, Randy*, he thought, *you can be so disgusting.*

But his tone made no impact. "So the answer's no," Randy jeered. "And I had all this faith in you."

"Get lost. I mean it." *You don't deserve an answer.*

"Don't wait too long," Randy said jauntily, unfazed, over his shoulder, as he headed off to the cafeteria.

He was sitting near the main entrance to the school one spring day after lunch, when a group of five men walked by and headed for the principal's office. They were all dressed in suits, and two of them in front were wearing American Legion hats.

He asked Josh Seybold, who was sitting next to him, what was going on, but he didn't know either.

The men vanished through the opaque office door, marching almost, rather than walking, deadly intense on accomplishing something.

It took two days to find out what had happened, Randy telling him the details before Sociology. A teacher named Mr. Fitzgerald, a popular instructor and track coach, had been suspended for saying some things in class about the Vietnam war, things that got back to a few parents. Then the Legion got wind of the statements and came to school to get him canned.

For the next week the school vibrated with rumors: Fitzgerald was being fired, he was resigning and not being fired, he was being reinstated, he was not going to be allowed to coach track, he was going to be given a job in the junior high school, his wife was suing the head of the school board. The rumors became so ludicrous no one could believe anything, and there was even a joke making the rounds, that Fitzgerald had gotten Mrs. Wright, the aging art teacher, pregnant.

The matter was settled when Mr. Fitzgerald showed up the following week to teach. Over the intercom during home-room period, however, the principal read a statement saying students should be aware that when teachers talked to them about controversial subjects, the teacher's views weren't those of the school system, and that they needed to evaluate all views carefully.

When he saw Randy again, at lunch, he asked him what he thought of the whole incident. He knew Randy had Mr. Fitzgerald for a teacher.

"He's lucky he didn't get the ax," Randy answered.

"No, that's not what I mean. Do you think the school board was fair?"

"Who cares? If he gives me a C for a mid-term he got what he deserved. If he gives me a B, the Legion didn't have any business sticking their asses in here." He started to snort in that sneery-singing way that was uniquely his, but then he saw Mrs. Barnes, their teacher, looking in their direction. He settled for a smirk instead.

Predictable Randy, he thought, measuring everything in terms of himself, even if he appeared to be joking. *Sad*! *How sad*!

After the Fitzgerald incident he began to see some things differently, including black people, maybe because they were on television more, in demonstrations protesting wrongs. Practically every week now there was TV coverage of blacks marching in the streets somewhere in the U.S.

There were only three of them in his junior class: Wink, a shy, short guy; Jefferson, a pretty good student in Algebra; and Rosa, who had a locker near him, and whom he'd gotten fond of, because she always sparred with him.

"Hey, James," she'd say to him, "heard your brain's overflowin' again. Gotta do something about that." Or she'd goad him about his clothes: "Some carnival geek pick out that shirt for you?" He loved her sassiness and started to hit back. There was something special in their saying good morning to each other every day.

For a week, though, Rosa became sullen and morose, so that he had to edge up to her one day, to try to make conversation. When he asked if he'd said something to upset her, she gave him a grunty dismissal as he followed her down the hall.

"C'mon, Rosa, it's no good holding it in, whatever it is."

"Just forget it." But then she turned toward him, leaning back against the hallway wall in dejection. "You sure you want to hear this?"

She poured out pathetic words, that her parents had saved up money for a long number of years and now were trying to buy their first house. But none of the real estate agents in town were willing to deal with them since her father's and mother's speech patterns gave them away. Over the phone they were told there were no houses on the market, even though ads in the paper showed otherwise.

Not ready to jump to conclusions, he asked Rosa if her family might be reading things into what they heard, but Rosa faced him wearily. "We know about this stuff, James. It's slick prejudice. Same thing as being called a nigger."

He stood there a moment, trying to deal with what Rosa was saying. Nobody had ever challenged him this way, with the idea that people in his community would deliberately harm someone else because of their skin color. Things like that happened only in the south. Yet here was this friend who spoke from experience, who had no reason to doctor what she was saying.

"I'm sorry," he fumbled, and found himself asking if there was anything he could do. But then his sentences began to sound like something said at a funeral. Was he telling Rosa her family should give up, that human decency was now lying in rigor mortis at the local morgue?

Rosa was bitter: "Run for Congress when you get older. Make some laws that let us have our little bungalow like anybody else."

So he knew he couldn't help her, but she looked so beaten he wanted to hug her.

"Thanks for asking anyway," she said finally. "Gotta go to American Lit." After she took ten more steps down the hall, she turned back to him. "You're okay, James. It's not your fault."

Howard was seeing things differently too, in his unique way, in Howard's own way, he would have called it.

"They're not like us, are they?" his buddy announced over the phone one night.

They hadn't seen each other in a day and a half so he didn't have any context to fit Howard's thought into, till finally he figured out that he was talking about girls. And either his friend's conclusion came from being totally naive, or there was some super subtlety that only Howard had noticed in all of civilization.

"Well, yeah, How. I mean there are the obvious things, hips and breasts, right." He was thankful he was on the phone and didn't have to keep the amusement off his face.

Howard sensed he sounded stupid. "No, I mean they, when, uh...they think differently, don't they? They've got all these emotions."

"Did you and Jen have a fight or something?"

"Kind of. I said something wrong I guess."

"What exactly?"

"Well, that's the point. I don't know what I said, and when I asked her, she said it was so obvious she wasn't even going to tell me."

"You need to ask her again, How. She wants to be asked."

"I tried that. She's all tight-mouthed though."

Even though they were on the phone, he could picture Howard looking forlorn and helpless. "Keep asking," he told his friend, wanting to prop him up.

"But you see what I mean? We're supposed to talk, and then we say the wrong thing and so then we're not supposed to talk when they really want us to."

"She likes you, How. Just remember that."

Howard was the one who burst the news that Randy was in some kind of trouble, something to do with his hair being too long, he said, as he puffed down the hall toward them, as fast as he ever moved.

A chorus of *You're kidding!* instantly filled the corridor, and other students joined him and Heather and Josh Seybold.

"Monahan won't let him into Phy Ed if he doesn't get his hair cut shorter," Howard went on. "He says the long stuff is a distraction to other students."

"That's ridiculous," Heather started to say, when all conversation stopped. Randy was coming down the hall toward them, and they all didn't know whether to let on they were talking about him.

"You want to know what I'm gonna do, right?" Randy strode into the middle of the group, enjoying being the center of attention.

"What're your choices?" Josh asked what was on everyone's mind.

"Get it cut or keep it as is. If it's long, I don't get course credit, and I don't graduate next year."

"It's your hair! It's your right to wear it long."A senior, Tracy, was indignant for all of them.

Randy let his weight settle back as a sneer got onto on his face. "We all know that. This is all about that war, and Monahan doesn't want any protester perverts around him. He thinks I'm one."

They pressed him: He did want to graduate next year, though, didn't he?

Randy shrugged, but it seemed to James the offhand gesture was a little phony. He could read some cowering underneath his friend's tough posture.

Randy guessed he did want to graduate, but then he tantalized his listeners: He wasn't going to take any shit from Monahan.

"So what's it going to be?" Heather's eyes were full of excitement.

"Don't know," Randy said, but now his voice seemed cagey, as though he really did know. "I hear the principal's on Monahan's side. Gotta deal with that too."

The next day most of the students were outside the building at lunch, when they saw a local television station's news truck drive onto campus. Its crew got outside and went toward the building, but before they got there Mr. Singer, the school principal, was coming out to meet them. As the students crowded toward the activity, a reporter asked Mr. Singer if he intended to back up Mr. Monohan's order to keep Randy from attending gym class.

He certainly did, Mr. Singer said.

And did he think that long hair was the issue? the reporter followed up. Wasn't Monahan's real complaint about the symbolism of long hair, in relation to the Vietnam war?

"Absolutely not," Mr. Singer said immediately, too quickly, as if he'd rehearsed the phrase.

The reporter seemed poised to ask further questions, but at that point a car pulled up beside the television crew's truck. Josh Seybold was driving, and out of it came Randy, smiling like a celebrity, and striding forward.

"My God!" somebody whispered.

"Bald!" people started to say. "He's shaved his head completely!" two girls giggled outright.

As soon as Randy came closer, the reporter thrust a microphone into his face, asking if he was the Randy who was the subject of the school controversy. Randy cockily said he guessed he was, as he winked covertly to a group of sophomore girls looking on.

"So why did you shave your head?"

"The long hair was a distraction," Randy said slyly, the sun gleaming off his skinned skull. "So I cut it off." He looked at Singer confidently then announced he had to go soon or be late for P.E. "Sorry," he said acidly to the principal as he stepped in front of him in a dramatic exit, crowding him deliberately.

Randy gone, the reporter turned to Singer and asked what he was going to do, if anything. With Singer fumbling some words that didn't make any sense, the reporter asked him a last question: Was he going to let Randy finish the semester? He'd removed the distraction, after all.

"I...uh...guess."

With that the reporter turned back to the camera, and Singer returned to the building. As he did the reporter said into the camera, "The school administration seems to have been taken completely surprise. A student here, a junior named Randy Fahey, seems to have made the school system look silly by playing their own game better than they could."

For days afterward, Randy was the hero of the school. Guys hung around him wherever he went, and girls, Heather included, moved in close to him when he was around, as though he were the only guy in the school. Randy took advantage of their admiration, teasing them with a flirty arrogance.

He thought no girl ever looked as smashing as she did that night.

Heather and he, and Howard and Jennifer, were at Heather's house, getting their pictures taken. She hadn't shown him her dress beforehand, and when he saw her come into the living room, he just stood there, awed with her appearance. She'd done her hair differently, and her new look made it seem as though he'd been set up out of the blue with a Hollywood starlet.

"Your mouth is open, Silly," she said, poking him in the ribs.

She was the talk of the junior prom. Even Randy, whose current girlfriend was terrifically striking, told him he was jealous, and three times during the dance at the gym he abandoned his date and cut in on him and Heather.

She was happy to let James share her triumph, hanging onto his arm more tightly than ever when people came up to her to compliment her. Later, outside the dance in the parking lot, she kissed him coyly, telling him her perfume was stronger in certain places. He just had to look for it.

But her prom triumph created small electric static between them, too, though he didn't know exactly why. And then came a time in mid-June where he could sense the same thing more definitely. It came at the lake where he and his dad fished, where a lot of kids had been hanging out after graduation week.

A party of seniors was drinking beers as they pulled up, got out and struck up conversations. When somebody gave him a beer, he took it without much enthusiasm since it was warm and bad-tasting. Then in the middle of a sip someone thrust a burning object under his nose and told him to take a toke.

"A what?"

"A toke, dummy." Sam Harralson was laughing a goofy laugh. "A drag. Do you good, man. Go on."

A bleached blond named Crystal, chimed in. "It's dope. You know, marijuana! Makes you high, James." She took the mauled cigarette from Sam and inhaled it, curling the corners of her mouth and sucking in large quantities of smoke.

He told them he'd pass for now, not sure of what to do. Later he saw Heather trying the cigarette, and he went over to her, protective and yet curious about her present state.

"C'mon, James, have a hit." She seemed different, her voice lower and velvety as she held the thing in front of his face. It was smaller now, and someone had stuck a safety pin through it, so whoever was inhaling could hold it.

"Maybe next time," he said. "Thanks anyway."

"Always cautious," she said. "Safe old James." She reached out as he started to turn away, touching his arm warmly.

He squeezed her hand instead, bothered by his own prudery in a sense and yet edgy about what Heather and the others were doing. He didn't like the idea of being out of control. Some of his friends were taking strange chemicals lately, and messing up their lives—letting their grades slip and getting into trouble on weekends. *Their choices, but bad choices?*

He drifted over to talk to Howard, steady How whose shyness and lack of confidence would keep *him* out of trouble forever, he thought. Howard was busy tucking in his shirt again, a constant ritual in the latest cycle of weight-gain and reduction he was on the losing side of.

"She doesn't like you as much now, does she?"

"Heather?" He was surprised at the frankness he was hearing.

Howard wet his lips: "She does but she doesn't." Then he gulped, letting his glance slide away, afraid that he'd crossed a line he shouldn't have. He waited another second, typically unsure about whether to continue.

"It's confusing," Howard said, when he saw he should go on. "You two, you just don't seem, well—I'm sorry, James. I shouldn't have said anything."

"Thanks, How," he told him. "I'm glad you did." It struck him that his friend was about as close to being a brother as any guy could be. It was family, after all, who told you what you didn't want to face.

Summer came, a series of days so free of responsibility, he felt he'd been born into a foreign country with a thinner, rarefied atmosphere.

With summer came the freedom to fall willy-nilly into his old habits with books. While his friends saw the warm, post-school days as a time to set aside reading matter, during the long vacations he filled his room with library books. He'd take out so many he couldn't remember which ones were due when, and his dad and Wendy would make bets with one another on how much his overdue library fines would be per month.

He paid the fines willingly, grateful for every idea or experience in the volumes he pored through. This vacation he was reading mysteries for the first time, and three European novels, half a dozen more books on architecture, and a work he found show-offish and full of strange energy at the same time, "On the Road." He couldn't believe the people in the book would ever act like that, like tame horses suddenly breaking out the sides of barns.

With summer, too, came long evenings with Heather, sensuous, easy nights.

Toward the end of school, during final exam week, he'd been troubled by her coming up to him in the hall one day and thrusting her opened palm into his face. Baffled, he asked her what he was supposed to see, and she held her palm up a second time, still leaving him in the dark. Then she gave a cutesy explanation, that she and her friend Tracy had cheated in old Miss Rudolph's class by inking answers onto their hands.

But the tension between them, from that incident and the marijuana episode at Potter's Lake, melted away in the warming degrees of July and August, when they would regularly drive to the lake in their free time, and sit in a grove of cottonwood trees they'd begun to think of as their own. There, listening to music on a portable radio, cooled by the lake water air currents, it was the first time he understood that doing nothing with someone could be as precious as doing something.

At home summer infused some tranquility. Not that Wendy had stopped playing her music, but now there was accommodation, and somehow their mother had gotten past her spells of the past winter, finding new resources in dealing with her daughter. One day in late August, when the outdoor temperatures were high enough to ignite tempers for the slightest reason, he witnessed his mom work a charm on his sister, a simple but useful charm, in the laundry room.

It began in a roundabout way with his mother asking Wendy why she continued to play a certain record when her dad was around.

"Mom, it's just music. We've been over this a zillion times."

"But that anti-war song, you know how touchy your dad is about all that."

Till now it was a familiar start to a familiar argument, but something caught his attention, some tone in his mother's voice that was altered. And then the course of her discussion took a new route too. "How about if I buy you that new blouse you want? a going-back-to-school gift? In exchange for your not playing that political stuff that bugs your dad so."

"Mom, this is bribery! I'm surprised at you." Wendy's answer took a while to surface, and he knew she was as shocked as him, listening from a distance. He could picture his sister's expression, going from a teenager's scowl to a young adult's amazement.

Then his mother said something that he never thought would have come from her mouth, a strange admission from her, the moral church-goer: "Moms bribe their daughters all the time, Wendy. Don't worry about it. Hand me those folded socks. And you can play that song as many times as you want, when Dad and I aren't here."

He met his sister as she was coming up the stairs. "You hear that?" she said. "I can't believe it. Mom's buying me off!"

"So refuse the blouse, Miss Purity!"

"Shut up, jerk. Oooh, I'll look so good in it!" she squealed.

Harris Point, Fall 1966–Summer 1967

As fine as the summer was, he was thrilled to be back in the classroom in September. He had Mrs. Bingham for Honors English, America Lit, and she would challenge his imagination, forcing him to defend what he said: "What about these sit-ins, James, these actions blacks are taking to open up public facilities? Would Thoreau advocate that?"

He told her yes, but Thoreau's method might take forever. A government law could make a quick change that would otherwise take years.

"But won't that cause people to subvert the law? If people had little part in making it?"

He had to admit it would, but she prodded him to not give up on his argument, to come back next day with a better response. She kept after him to be the best he could.

His love of learning got more fuel when he and his parents drove to the state university to visit the campus, where a volunteer student showed them the buildings and landmarks: the student union on the lakefront, the libraries, athletic facilities and the liberal arts cluster where he would take most of his classes. In the center of the campus was a large area with a fountain at its center. From this pedestrian mall ran a street, a mile long, to the city's square, in the middle of which sat the state capitol building.

The size of the campus stunned him. So many buildings and students! All of them filled with the business of learning! It was as though the whole world had nothing to do but consider ideas all day long.

He sat in on a history lecture, trying not to look conspicuous. But the large number of students, three hundred or more, soon made him feel comfortably anonymous. He felt intrigued by the train of thought the professor was developing, and he couldn't understand why a student two rows ahead of him seemed to be falling asleep.

The library was so huge it was almost like a skyscraper. Inside it he'd been struck by the number of books it held, thousands of them with millions of new ideas!

Out in the mall later, going to meet his parents, he saw students at tables distributing literature about various causes, and there seemed to be camaraderie among the groups, women with pamphlets about women's health, black and white students with tracts about equal rights for black people, a cluster of people with a petition for legalizing marijuana. On the cement rim of a fountain at the mall's edge two guitarists sat, entertaining a small group of onlookers. He'd never seen a place like this, where seriousness and casual, good feeling seemed to mix so easily.

Back home he tried to convey his lingering enthusiasm to Heather, but her reaction was half-hearted. She told him then, for the first time, that she wasn't going on to school like he assumed, at least not in the near future, and he checked his excitement. Maybe her family couldn't afford to send her to college, he thought. She had five brothers and sisters, after all.

He edged away from the topic at the time, not sure how to open it up again, or when to.

Going on to school was on the minds of more than a few of his classmates, but for some of them in an unusual way, which he found out one day when he strolled into the locker room after school. There he heard one of his cross-country teammates ask Dave Norman which college he was going to, a strange question since neither of the Norman twins had ever mentioned anything about going on after high school. Then Dave said, "Haven't the foggiest idea where I'm headed!"

"You're just doin' it so you don't have to go to Vietnam?"

"Why not?"

"And you just decided yesterday?"

"Yeah. My dad's been telling me about the president's big troop buildup. The only way out of it, he says, is going on to school."

He heard a third voice added to the conversation, Jason Kendall's he thought: "Real patriotic, man!"

"Hey," Dave came back, "do you even know where Vietnam is? I mean, could you pick it out on a map, for crissake?"

"No, but–!"

"My dad told me some students over there set fire to our whatchamacallit, the, uh–where our diplomats are."

"The embassy," the unidentified voice put in.

"Why'd they do that?" It was Jason again.

"Who knows?" Dave finished. "Hey, I'm feelin' good today. Like I could place first or second maybe."

The Vietnam war was affecting everything lately. There'd been a recent secret meeting of the Board of Deacons of their church, a meeting held in the back room of a local restaurant, where the Board was going to decide whether Reverend Allen should continue having the congregation pray for people in foreign lands. A strong faction of the deacons said the practice could mean foreign enemies weren't really enemies.

When Reverend Allen showed up, having found out about the meeting, tempers got untethered, and two of the deacons accused him of the worst motives, calling him a communist sympathizer.

Wendy and he, quietly coming in the house after a nighttime school function, found that the restaurant argument had flown home. Their dad was shouting—actually shouting at their mother!—that Reverend Allen was collaborating. There was a war on after all, and people had to take sides, dammit! The deacons had every reason to feel the way they did!

His mother's voice was alternately angry and pleading: "It's just a phrase, Ralph. He wants us to be understanding of others."

"There's no place in the pulpit for that!"

"Oh don't take out your frustrations on him. If the war's gone sour, that's one thing—"

"The war's going just fine, Janine!" his dad thundered. "Just fine!"

Wendy and he, conspiring, decided to slip outside and come back in, deliberately noisy, as though coming in for the first time. Doing that had the right effect, of ending the argument then and there.

But next day his dad's anger burst out again, in a tirade against Wendy's music, in this case a new rock group who had no political songs at all. Even after Wendy toned the volume way down his dad went on, raving that she probably had some records by that creepy new guy who went on stage with snakes around his neck and dressed like a vampire. The world had gone off the deep end. Kids today didn't have any sense at all.

Now it was his father instead of his mother who'd taken on the crusade against the new culture.

Right after that, too, his dad reversed himself about acting on his political beliefs. In the sporting goods store front window was a brand new item: **Vietnam: Support Our Troops!**

"Like my new sign, James?" his father asked, when he came inside the store on his way home from school.

He reminded his dad about his statement a long time back, that business and politics didn't mix. You could lose business by supporting a cause.

"Sometimes you have to take a stand, son." Ralph Brandes blew a dust particle off the sign, proud of his new possession.

"But I've got to study tonight," he told her.

"You never want to have fun anymore," Heather humphed.

They were in her parents' kitchen, after dinner, perfecting an argument they'd been having for the last two months. Usually both of them would bend: She'd let him go home and study for an hour or two, then he'd return to her house for "fun." Then he'd go back home at ten. But tonight he really didn't have to study, and yet he found himself saying that he did, and he didn't care. He was just tired of the ritual and knew he was being dishonest, which bothered him, but only up to a point.

He didn't like the confusion, but he disliked their boring old disagreement even more, and maybe he even disliked her, if only this time. He had a right to be moody too, once in a while.

Their being together hadn't been easy lately, as though outsiders were around all the time, but they themselves were the outsiders.

When he'd finally asked if she didn't want to talk about going on to college because her parents couldn't afford it, she scoffed away his suggestion. What on earth made him think she wanted to go to college in the first place?

In her studying this semester she was doing just token work to get D's or low C's, on top of which she was blaming her teachers for her own lack of effort. When he told her that was what she was doing, she didn't speak to him for two days.

He couldn't talk about anything serious with her. All she wanted to do was gossip about who was seeing who in school, and sometimes he felt himself drooping under her trivia. His shoulders sagged from it.

Now, with Thanksgiving past, he thought back to a year before, when he'd been excited about buying her a Christmas gift. This year he'd do likewise, but he was thinking in terms of "have to" rather than "want to."

Wendy, who was having her own first romance, read his anxiety and told him to talk things out with Heather. But he couldn't imagine talking would solve anything. *Words, useless words.*

Randy tried to help too, or so he first thought: "Hey, James, you need to get to Stacy Mohs."

"Do she and Heather share a lot?" He thought Randy was suggesting Heather's sometime friend as a mediator.

"Hell no, James. She just broke up with her boyfriend over in Paine Hollow. She's available again. And ripe."

Big help, he thought. (Maybe he'd even muttered it aloud). *Thanks, Randy, but no thanks. Ripe? My god!*

More college catalogs kept arriving in the mail, and he and his mom visited another school, a private college whose architecture fascinated him. But he didn't feel the excitement there that he'd felt at the state university. The place was too quaint.

Visiting the college, though, he felt once more the distance he'd soon be putting between himself and his Harris Point world. His family, his friends at high school, the places he spent time at—all that seemed to be shrinking in his mind. His present days were more and more cast forward to his upcoming life on a campus.

One part of Harris Point was even stronger in his mind, however, Howard, who was awfully grumpy lately, and avoiding most of his friends. Everyone speculated that the trouble was romantic, but he knew better. If anything Jennifer and his friend were even closer.

Nobody—Randy, Heather, the Normans, or Josh Seybold, who lived on Howard's block—could figure out Howard's withdrawal.

Until his dad mentioned what he'd found out that week, that Howard's dad had lost his job, again, a month before.

Norm Parker's work history seemed haunted. Twice in the last five years he'd been employed by places that closed. And now, where he worked, the retail center was being taken over by a national chain. Swooping into town, the corporate heads weren't just trimming but scything down whole departments, and Norm Parker was among the discarded chaff.

His dad told how cruel it had all been. The bosses had just come in and said that twenty people were fired then and there. As compensation they were each given a free meal certificate to the local pancake house—free flapjacks to make you feel better about losing your job, his dad said.

No wonder Howard was the way he was these days! And he was probably upping his part-time job hours to help keep the family afloat.

What to do, he thought later. *You just don't leave old friends fending for themselves, James.*

So he called Howard and edged his way into the topic of the senior Parkers. From there he mentioned (as casually as possible) he'd heard about the family's misfortune. And from there he tried an elliptical "if you need anything, How, I'll be happy to..." *Don't be too obvious with your sympathy or it will look like pity.*

"You worry too much about us, James." Howard's recent grumpiness seemed to be back, and he felt that he'd been off target, but then he heard the old Howard: "Maybe we could hit a movie this weekend, okay? Just you and me, not Jen and Heather?"

"Sure. I'd like that. You sound tired."

"I am. I've been working a lot. Have to. Well you know why, you can guess."

His "uh-huh" didn't seem adequate, but it filled seconds while he got his emotions collected. His chest ached for his friend.

"I appreciate this, James. I really do."

"Listen, How, it's nothing."

"No, I really mean it."

As Howard's family humpty-dumptied off the wall, a rumor circulated that Randy's father was transforming a small inheritance into a larger fortune. A part of the rumor, at least, had to be true since the Faheys were moving to a new, huge home in the outlying suburbs.

Before Randy left the neighborhood there was one last time when he let himself be with the guys he'd grown up with, a basketball game on a warm March day, which brought out the classic Randy Fahey they'd liked and barely tolerated at the same time.

High energy Randy. Competing like every point would turn the whole game. Playing all out, non-stop. He had shakers-and-movers energy, Harris Point's football coach once pointed out, before Randy quit the team when he couldn't play first string quarterback as a sophomore.

Scrapper Randy, whose elbow in Howard's solar plexus stopped the game momentarily, the score tied nineteen all, with twenty going to be the game-winner. When Howard barely had his breath back, Randy badgered him to play on. "Okay, buddy? Ready?"

"Okay," Howard said, but it was clear he didn't really want to start yet.

Take-no-prisoners Randy. Butting Howard out of the court a minute later in a melee for a loose rebound. After Randy flipped the ball back to Josh, expecting it to be flipped back to him, so he could sink the game-winner, he was furious at what happened next, at Josh handing the ball over to the opposing side.

"Hey! What're you doing? Jesus!" Randy huffed as he stormed toward his teammate.

"It's theirs," Josh said simply, turning away. "You pushed Howard out of there under the board."

"What? I never touched him!"

"You did too," Howard said, his lip pouty and his nose drippy.

"It's ours," Dan Norman agreed.

Three dribbles and a shot later, Dan won the game for the other side.

The ball was no sooner through the net than Randy was calling for a new game with new sides. "C'mon," he said, "one more, we've got time!"

There was one more game, too, which Randy's side won, making it possible for him to be a regular guy afterwards, by offering Howard a "sorry" for the elbow in his chest. Triumphant, he could be apologetic, in a lordly way.

"No problem," Howard said, but James was pretty sure that Howard was still going to remember what had happened. And later his best buddy told him he wasn't sad about Randy leaving the local streets for good.

All day at work, at Stuffy's Pizza Palace, he'd been thinking about what he had to do soon. Heather would be upset, but what else could he do? He had to be honest about what he felt.

He just didn't enjoy being with her any longer. She was attaching herself more and more to a crowd that only wanted to have fun, and she always wanted him to join her. But he found her friends uninteresting, and they themselves rarely talked about anything for long.

He made the mistake again, last week, of asking what she'd do after graduation, and she got angry, saying she didn't know what she'd do, and she didn't care. He should stop getting after her about it.

When he picked her up at eight, each of them was gloomy in their separate ways. They sat in front of her house trying to figure out what to do that evening, but his mind was on how he'd bring up the subject of their splitting.

In the middle of a long silence, disquiet floating freely, she was the one who brought things into the open. "You want to break up with me, don't you?" she said, as if she wanted to settle some score.

"No. Well, I just think..., uh, we don't seem to have good times now, together."

"It was so good at first," she said mournfully, her mood softening.

"Maybe we could do some things we did back then," he offered, but he knew he didn't want to. He cracked the car window in case he had to think more clearly—fresh air, lucid thoughts and all that, but there wasn't anything to decide really. *Nothing in common now.*

She let his idea go unanswered for a minute and then asked him: "Could we kiss one last time? Just so it ends like it should?" She was looking ahead, not at him, as she spoke. There was no need for complexity, just a call for a final caring for one another.

He leaned over and kissed her, with a tenderness that hadn't been in their embraces in months. Their eyes linked their separate sadnesses and relief.

Then she got out of the car and went back inside. As she did he felt the wetness she'd left on his cheek.

Within a month she was going out with Sam Harralson, and he could have felt outraged at how quickly he'd been replaced. Instead he was glad to see her having the good time she wanted.

Salutatorian! He was going to be the salutatorian of his class. When he told his parents they were almost silly with pleasure.

What would he say in his speech, his mother pried, and he told her that was the best part, that only the valedictorian spoke at graduations.

"But you should too," his dad said. "I'll call the principal tomorrow."

"No, don't," he said. "Please!" He didn't want to give a speech at all.

"Yes, do, Ralph. No, don't! Oh, James, James, I'm so proud! You'll need a new suit." His mother was holding him, and his father was pounding him on the back, his only way of showing affection. "You'll be on stage, won't you? A Brandes up there in front of everybody! Imagine!"

On stage at graduation he was proud too, but near the end of the ceremony at one moment he was thinking ahead again and backwards simultaneously. Yes, he thought, there would be another ceremony like this sometime in the future. "You'll be the first in the family to have a college degree," his dad said on their visit to the university, and he actually strutted a bit when he said it.

But as he looked at his parents in the front rows, his father beaming as he had at the state U. more than a year and a half ago, a conversation came floating into his thoughts. It was an odd one in the way it kept poking away at his daily attention.

Late at night. Downstairs in the den, he was, with the door open at the top of the stairs. He could hear his mom and dad talking in the kitchen, and figured they must have thought he was upstairs in his room, where he'd carelessly left the music on.

A week after they'd visited the university.

His dad speaking: "I've been thinking. Suppose he wants to enlist rather than go on to school right away."

His mother amazed (as he was): "But why would he, Ralph?"

"The call to duty. It's not so hard to understand. Stu Leonard's son just went in."

"But give up college, when he's so bright?"

"He could serve now and then go on to school. He'd have the GI bill, or whatever it is nowadays."

"Has he talked to you about this?" His mother's words full of worry. "Has he told you he wants to do this?"

"No, but I wouldn't be surprised if he does."

His mother didn't say anything for a moment. Then he heard her trying to get his dad to promise he wouldn't suggest anything, to leave their son alone.

His dad backed off, but one step forward after two back: "I'm just guessing he might want to enlist. This may be his only chance to prove himself for Uncle Sam. You need to think how you'd react if he told you."

"But he'll enlist just to please you." Alarm in his mother's sentences.

"He's a big boy, Janine."

"You'd love for him to do it, wouldn't you?"she said sharply, suddenly. Her words held a boring-in bitterness he'd never heard before. A moment later he heard her footsteps going toward the living room, and then he heard the television come on. In the kitchen his father was whistling softly.

Looking out from the stage now, at high school graduation, the prelude to his college years, he tried to sort things out: his father's present smiling face, in the crowd below him, vying with his father's voice, that early autumn, glorifying military service, as he, his son, overheard while not wanting to.

There seemed to be two versions of Ralph Brandes.

Which was the real one? What did his dad expect of him?

He had nothing better to do and it was his day off, so he found himself on the town's main street, watching the July Fourth parade. It was a cool summer, and the day was overcast again.

His dad, in uniform, marching with the American Legion, spotted him and gave him a perky, white-gloved thumbs-up sign. Seconds later, he saw a flashy convertible coming down the street, with a sign on its front saying

Harris Point Honors
PFC Gerald Parsons
Purple Heart, Vietnam

The black person on the back of the rear seat was doing a famous-person routine, acknowledging the crowds, when James heard a familiar voice behind him. "My god, your socks match for once."

He turned. "Rosa!" He hadn't seen his friend since school let out and was delighted to see her, and to feel her affectionate hand on the middle of his back. They chatted a moment about happenings in town.

"So what do you think of my hero brother?"

"I'm impressed, and I bet he gets his socks matched all the time." He thought he'd give her another opening for their old bantering bond.

But Rosa's face turned angry suddenly. "That's not one of those sick jokes, is it?"

"No, why?" *What on earth did I say?*

"Jesus, you don't know, do you? You haven't heard."

"I guess I don't. How about telling me?"

"Take a good look, James." She was pointing to the car. "Gerald only needs one sock. He lost a leg in LBJ's war."

"Oh my god!" And he started on a lengthy apology, but Rosa waved it away, as her brother, in the parade car, passed them. When she spoke there was bitterness in her voice, though she'd just smiled gamely at her celebrity sibling.

"They don't give purple hearts for winning bridge tournaments," she said, "and the worst thing is that Gerald loved to play basketball. No more pickup games in the park now."

"I'm sorry for you," he started in again. "For him too," and once more he tried to get out an apology, and yet again she let him know his goof was understandable. But he still felt awful: *God, James, you'd think you practiced insensitivity.* He wasn't sure if he should risk anything else with more words, so he did the next best thing, consoling Rosa with his hand on her shoulder.

"It's so damned sad,"she said. "Thanks, James." She covered his hand with hers.

Back home for lunch, an hour later, he came into the living room where his dad was reading the newspaper, and his father mentioned what a hero the Parsons boy was. A young man like that certainly did Harris Point and his family proud.

So much of his morning's embarrassment was still in his head, he didn't respond right away, which his dad picked up on.

"What is it, son?"

"I don't know, something Gerald Parsons' sister said to me, while we were watching the parade. Most of the fighting's being done by blacks and poor white people, and it doesn't seem fair."

"But he's served with honor, James."

Wendy, who had come into the room and been listening, suddenly was in the conversation:

"It's just that there are other issues, Dad."

"Like what? You either serve or you don't."

"Whether we belong over there, whether we're doing the right thing." Wendy's voice got meek as the words came out and she saw their father digging in.

"Of course we are! If we don't, the communists will take over."

It was his turn now. "But the South Vietnamese government doesn't seem to be very good. And last week there was that bit on TV, about the attack on our ships, at the start of the war. The military may have fabricated it."

His father suddenly glowered, alarming his sister and him. "Don't you listen to those damn liberal reporters, you two. They don't have any guts for this thing, and they never will. 'Fabricated'! That's just the kind of word they'd use." Having finished the paper, he rose from his chair, to leave.

There was a pulpy silence, then Wendy tried some smoothing over: "He's not saying he agrees with the reporters, Dad. He's just telling you what he heard. Isn't that right, James?"

"Yes," he said. After a moment, though, with their parent out of the room, he turned to Wendy, adding softly, "I guess."

He always thought later what he should have said. It nagged him that he didn't think quicker, that he had to plod through ideas. Right now, at work, with a big lull in customer orders, he put everything together the way it should have been.

What he should have told his dad was that it wasn't right that in places in the country blacks still couldn't vote or go to the same bathrooms as white people, yet they were the ones fighting the U.S. cause.

And here at home the Parsons family wasn't able to buy a house they'd saved for. No justice at all.

It wasn't just a question of somebody being obligated to serve their country because they were Americans. They had to be Americans with the same rights as everyone.

He thought he'd bring up the discussion sometime when his dad was in a good mood about the war, maybe soon, in fact, because American troops had just won some major battles, the TV was saying these days.

"And apparently with the inheritance money, he made a killing."

A day after their living room discussion, they were on less-strained ground, his dad enjoying his mother's peach pie, from the first of the summer crops: "Ed Rustin told me Herman Fahey invested in some western utilities, and the stocks nearly tripled in six months. Then he used half of that money to fund that big development out by Blue Springs. He's probably made half a million in the last two years."

"I suppose that's why they moved to that huge new house," his mother said.

"And that's why Randy's such an obnoxious guy now," Wendy pounced. She'd always disliked Randy, though she disliked a lot of people on principle these days, as a teen.

"Is that true, James?" The pie crust had fallen from his dad's fork, and he scooped up stray pieces.

"I don't see a lot of him these days. He runs with a different crowd now."

"Money's giving him a big head," Wendy followed up, "even bigger than before. I said hello to him downtown last week, and he acted like I was contaminated, for god's sake."

"Wendy!"

"Mom, we've been over this. I don't really mean God when I say that."

"It's God to me!"

"Anyway, he just started to walk by me. When I hollered hello to him, he tried to act like he hadn't seen me."

"Too bad," his mother said. "I used to like him. He could be real funny, I remember."

He picked up where Wendy left off: "This new crowd isn't any good for him–that's the sad thing. They're wild, maybe even into shoplifting for fun, the rumor is."

"Good that he doesn't try to see you then, James," his dad offered. "Can I have more pie, Janine?"

She handed him the serving dish. "Too bad all that wealth couldn't have come to Howard's family."

No one could disagree with that.

Twice a week, at practice and on game night, he watched his Little League players regularly crash into each other, drop easy fly balls, and fling wild throws across the diamond. By the third week of the season he had an irrational thought: The team might be trying to lose, to make ineptitude a way of life. He felt he was on his way to becoming Laughing Stock Coach of the Year.

At the end of the third game, as his players were leaving the field, he was sitting on the bench, collecting gear and pondering what to do. Should he come down hard on all his players or find one or two halfway promising ones to nurture as leaders? Or should he…?

"Maybe you shouldn't worry that they're a bunch of total klutzes," he heard behind him.

"What?" he said, turning. It was as though thoughts had sprung out of his head, against his will. Someone was publicly voicing the ghastly truth.

"The kids are having a good time. Why worry about it, if they're not?"

A moment later he was shaking hands with Eugene Fitzgerald, Harris Point history teacher and parent of second baseman Tim Fitzgerald.

He hadn't been in any of Fitzgerald's classes, but he knew his students liked him. Almost all of them had been angry when the school board had tried to oust him, and some had even tried to start a petition supporting him.

"I've been watching for a couple of innings," Fitzgerald went on. "I've never seen a group of kids so unworried about their lack of success. But they love being together. They're having a ball out there."

Fitzgerald's friendly expression was an invitation to open up, and he found himself in that situation of spilling all to a stranger. As a coach he was supposed to succeed, and he wasn't sure his Hawks would win a single game. They might not even come close in fact, and it was embarrassing.

"Only if you let it be," Fitzgerald pointed out. "Look, I'm the only parent who showed up today, so these kids don't have big success models at home. And consider yourself lucky. Those absentee moms and dads could be out here pestering you."

The thought had a certain attraction, and he found himself remembering what his fellow students frequently mentioned: Fitzgerald was a fast mind with unusual insights.

He told him he'd consider the idea and thanked him for the suggestion. He'd think about it.

"Don't think too much," Fitzgerald said. "It's summer, after all. We're supposed to be loose and easy, which this team seems to know better than we do."

The next week in practice, he saw what Fitzgerald meant. Going through the motions of being ballplayers, his team was enjoying a low-energy togetherness, and baseball seemed merely an excuse for dawdling through July and August. If one of them happened to connect with a hit or make a good fielding play, the others would do the required clapping and back-patting. But what was important were their random conversations on and off the field. More than one error happened because two players were late in breaking off yakking to one another.

That same week Fitzgerald pointed out something else: the Hawks' outfield was full of nature-loving dreamers, kids who seemed half a state away but who also were enthralled in the long stretches of mown grass. "Henry David Thoreau now playing in right field;" Fitzgerald nasaled out, imitating a major-league announcer; "in center, Ralph Waldo Emerson; in left, John Muir."

Fitzgerald became a bench fixture, next to him, and he began to realize the man showed up because he enjoyed their talks. While the Hawks kicked away grounders and flailed at wild pitches, the two of them rambled through more ideas than he ever thought existed, from Fitzgerald's notion that baseball was a farmer's sport for poets, to his own idea that the tract houses being built in town were an insult to architecture. Fitzgerald was a free-ranging thinker, and his enthusiasm for thought rubbed off.

On game days the opposing team's coaches and parents would see them as oddball jokes in the baseball world, as he—they, really—coached as little as possible. But it didn't matter, they were so enjoying the continuous bench dialogue they'd established. The team, too, liked Fitzgerald's being around since it lowered James' expectations for them even more.

By game five, he'd given up all hope of the team winning any games. The conclusion was just a fact, though, not a badge of shame. Everyone—the kids, Gene Fitzgerald, and himself—settled just fine into life in the league's cellar.

When Howard came in to order a super-large pepperoni, he made the mistake of asking who he was going to share it with. Howard told him, sheepishly, no one.

Dumb question, he told himself. *Think before talking, James, once in awhile anyway.*

He recalled the recent time when the two of them had gone to the movie together, just the two of them without girlfriends. They'd shared a large bag of popcorn, and while he randomly took bites, Howard kept up a steady digging, into the bag. At a restaurant later, they laughed when How reached in his shirt pocket for a piece of paper and pulled out four popcorn kernels with it. That was the great thing about Howard, a lack of pretenses that came with his frequent shortage of couth.

Sometime in those moments, that night, he imagined Howard (and maybe Jennifer with him) in later life, surrounded on a cement patio with children, dogs, barbecue apparatus, blue plastic wading pools, tricycles and anti-mosquito gadgets on poles stuck into the edge of the nearby driveway. Howard would be blithely setting fire to hot-pads, he thought, but enjoying the company and working on his fifth beer and tenth chicken wing. Potato chips would be flying in the wind like escapee parakeets, and his friend would be grinning like he owned the whole neighborhood if not the state, country and world.

He had good memories of Randy, too, he recalled, but only in time too far back. Once especially, when they were in the tenth grade and playing catch in front of Randy's house, they'd spent an hour perfecting their throws, picking up the pace, and challenging each other with a greater level of skill. The better they got, the more they were heady with one another, taking pride in their own and the other's accomplishments, egging one another on.

In a special exhaustion they sat on Randy's porch later, and it was then that Randy shared feelings he would never share again, of a loneliness he felt now, from his parents. His father was working all the time, and his mother had a new social calendar that kept her away from home. He envied James's having a sister; he always wanted one.

He was jealous of James's ability to make friends so easily. Oh, he had friends too, but he wasn't really sure if the ones he had would be there tomorrow because of his way of moving into a crowd and demanding attention. But he couldn't stop himself. It was just the way he was. When he was young his dad always encouraged him to be that way.

There were troubles between his mom and dad too, that nobody else knew about. He didn't know what it was all about, but he was afraid.

Afraid. Randy afraid! It was almost impossible to believe these days.

These days Randy was out of his life, but when he appeared, rarely, he brought with him a brash self-confidence that seemed inborn.

A quick memory flash: of his being at the mall and getting into his car, when he saw a new yellow convertible heading across the parking lot toward him. In the afternoon sunlight he couldn't make out the driver and his companion for a while, but then he saw who it was.

"What say, ol' man?" Randy pulled up and let the big engine throttle down. In the rider's side was a girl he didn't know, who looked annoyed at their having stopped.

"Nice wheels. Yours or your dad's?"

"His, but I let him know when he can drive it." Randy looked momentarily over to his chic companion, as if to cue her, and the girl gave him a quick approving look before tending her notice-me image more, in the visor mirror.

"Where you workin' this summer, James?"

He started to answer, but Randy revved the engine so that his words were drowned. He thought about repeating them but figured it was wasted effort.

The noise came down enough for Randy's goodbye: "Gotta go," he said. "People are waiting for us at the country club. Be seeing ya."

He knew enough not to compete with the engine again, and he waved as the convertible screeched away, the girl's hair streamlined in the wind and sunlight.

It was hard not to be envious. It was sad, though, a friend putting so much distance between them. And he recalled that earlier afternoon after they drilled wonderful baseball throws at one another and Randy opened up. Was all that uncertainty gone? There was so much of it there once, and he didn't think that in Randy's new surroundings, the posh suburbs, it had all gone away. It couldn't have.

Howard and Randy, one wealthy and the other just getting by. He wished some of the wealth could be shifted to the other. After all why were the cards of wealth dealt so erratically in life? On the other hand Howard by some quirk of luck was his own person, while Randy might still be years finding his way in the shadow of his dad's new money. Howard and Randy, poor and rich. *Or maybe the other way around, in a way.*

He was washing his mom's Plymouth before dinner, when his dad drove up in his own car. Out of the Buick, he walked over and stood closer than he usually did, with a stern look.

"So you and Gene Fitzgerald are buddies now!" he accused. "Is that right?"

Taken aback and not knowing what his dad was getting at, he stabbed at a reply: "We chat at the Hawks' games."

"He sits on the bench the whole game?"

"Yeah. What's this all about, Dad?"

"Edddie Finch told me. He saw Fitzgerald there at a game last week, when he picked up his youngest kid."

He waited for his dad to go on, but all he got was an on-going glare. So he tried more talk:

"He's the only team parent who ever comes to a game, and the team's a disaster."

Still no luck, his dad unreadable, so he went on: "Our innings are real long. That's the way it is with losers, and it's nice to have someone to talk to." He let the ideas register then finished: "And I like the guy, if you want to know."

His dad opened up finally: "You know the school board tried to fire him!"

"For being honest about his views, I heard." *So it's the war!*

Ralph Brandes' forehead went scarlet. "He talks to you about Vietnam then, doesn't he? He does! I know it."

Now the source of his father's anger became clear, and he almost relished what he was about to say, but then he felt some sympathy, because his dad was going to be disappointed with the truth. "We've never discussed the war at all," he said simply.

When he told his dad this, his reaction was almost comic but in a sad way, like a look from a prize-fighter suddenly told by the referee that the fight was over because his shoe was untied. "Well," his dad said, nervous now, "I just wanted to, uh..." Then he turned away.

Again, he thought. *It's happened again.*

The previous year, when they'd visited the university, there had been ugly moments in the otherwise pleasant day on campus.

He'd come from visiting that class, back to the mall where those tables were set up and students were distributing literature. But in the middle of the area his dad was making a scene while his mother desperately tried to control him.

At a table separate from the others were two men and two women behind a sign saying "DRAFT RESISTOR INFORMATION. OUT OF VIETNAM NOW!"

His father was pointedly standing near the table and saying aloud, "Goddamn draft dodgers!" deliberately putting enough volume into his voice to be heard by passers-by and the people at the table. His mother was rushing toward the scene.

"Just calm down, Ralph, please. You're embarrassing me, and here comes James."

"I don't care if I am," his father hissed. "No son of mine's coming to a place like this."

"Your son's got a good head on his shoulders, Ralph," Janine Brandes reminded him. "He's going to be in classes, not out here with these people. Now stop."

His father took some deep breaths. "You're right," he admitted. Still, turning away from the tables and strolling up to him, his son, he gloated quietly. "Told them a thing or two, didn't I, Son?"

"Ralph, don't start again." His mom was behind them, advancing quickly, to muzzle her husband if need be.

"I won't, Janine. Just think, James, you'll be the first in the family to have a college degree." Mixed into his doting look was another glance over his shoulder, to see if he could open up his attack once again, on the odd chance that his wife had evaporated.

Two weeks later, at the Hawks' last game of the season, Gene Fitzgerald didn't show up until the fourth inning, and then he was a crustacean, brooding at the bench's far end. The Hawk players, sensing a change, kept an edgy space between him and themselves. Even Fitzgerald's son remained distant.

In school friends told him Mr. Fitzgerald had days when he'd scowl all day long, a murky, hard personality best avoided. But he'd never actually seen him in such a state till this afternoon. Not knowing how to deal with it, he let the older man mull his thoughts.

When the game ended, Fitzgerald sat there momentarily on the bench, staring into the dust at his feet. Rousing himself, he moved to where James was stuffing bats into a bag, and there he made regrets for his offish mood. "I haven't told you," he said. "I get depressed. Not just down but down for days. I've got a counselor now, for the trouble, the attacks. They're more frequent, lots."

Feeling sympathy, he offered help, an invitation to listen, to let Fitzgerald talk things out. But the man's reflex was to raise his arms in a weak despair. Talk, he said, was a problem. His wife thought he talked his way into deeper depression. His counselor thought talk was the only way to escape it.

"Does it matter what you talk about?" He was curious as well as supportive.

"I read things," Fitzgerald said wearily. "I think about them. I can't let go of what bothers me. I dwell too much, my shrink says."

"But can you stop it even if you wanted to?"

Fitzgerald answered as though he'd not followed his question. He was off somewhere in his own labyrinth: "There's this place called Khe Sanh. In this article I read Thursday—or was it Tuesday? Hell, it doesn't matter, the date."

"The place sounds like some kind of resort," he said, mostly to keep the conversation going.

Fitzgerald switched into a sarcastic litany: "Hardly! Over in Vietnam, over in that great field-test of our military, that proving ground of the magnificent struggle between ugly old communism and capitalism, over there is this outpost we're defending. It's a hell-hole like those of us in Korea never saw. Maybe nothing like it was in World War Two. Our troops are surrounded there, and we hold it day after day."

"Courageously?" He couldn't tell where Fitzgerald was going with his train of thought.

"Bravely, courageously, all the adverbs you can find like that," Fitzgerald jeered. "But no one seems to be able to explain the importance of the place. We send men in there to die, in that resort, as you called it, and—! And this war goes on because it's an idea, but there's no way out once in, and here I am talking my way into depression again. Damn, my wife's right." He stopped, one hand shaking as though fed by voltage.

He didn't know whether to draw Fitzgerald out more or steer him to less agitating territory. He chose the latter: "I didn't know you were you in Korea. My dad was too."

Fitzgerald took a series of deep breaths, and at the end of them, he looked up, baring the red outlines of his eyes. "That's why the school board couldn't fire me," he said slowly. "I was a veteran."

Abruptly, the man rose and strode to his car, where he reached in to get a package, which he came back with. From the bag he withdrew a copy of a book, as finely bound a book as James had ever seen. "I wanted you to have this," Fitzgerald said, a bit shyly, as he handed it over."It's Toqueville's 'Democracy in America,' a classic."

Now it was his turn to be looking for proper words. "You didn't have to," he started to say, his fingers feeling the fine texture of the book's cover. The work was almost so beautiful that he feared soiling it by opening it. And he was thinking what a fitting symbol it was, this volume honoring the times he and this man had spent together this summer.

"There's an inscription," Fitzgerald told him.

He opened the cover and read

For James, a fine mind,
a great (unconventional) coach.
Gene

"It's beautiful," he said. "Thanks again. They shook hands, a lingering, longer-than-average clasp, and then walked off the field together.

He was sad that they would have no further discussions, but he knew that he would hear Fitzgerald's probing, cajoling, prodding voice in his mind, in his college years, as he tackled textbooks, wrote papers, and discussed ideas in classes.

Probably, he thought, he should tell his father about this discussion touching upon Vietnam. But he knew he wouldn't. *Pointless to tell. Dangerous too, to Dad's stability.* Gene Fitzgerald wasn't alone in not being able to deal with the war.

The Norman brothers were heading off to separate schools in Ohio, Randy was bound for an expensive small college in the north, Josh

Seybold was landing in academe in Boston, and Howard would be commuting to a community college twenty miles away.

A week before they would all separate, they drove out to a lake one night and had a going-away party for themselves.

He felt bad for Howard, that he wouldn't be having the same opportunities as the rest of them, but Howard took the whole thing in stride. "We'll be together at Thanksgiving," he said, though he and they knew this wouldn't be the case.

Randy would show up only near eleven, with two of his new friends in tow. He stayed only a short time, though they'd all arranged their free-time schedules for the whole evening around him.

"Is this going to be fun, James, this college thing?" Dan Norman asked as they watched a pair of fishermen in a lanterned boat fifty yards out from the beach.

"I can't wait," he said, "but this is nice too, all of us here."

"What about this draft thing people are talking about? Maybe we won't be in college after all. We'll be over in those rice paddies in Asia."

"It wouldn't be so bad in one way. At least it would be everybody's war, not just something fought by blacks and poor people."

Dan was finding humor in the moment, and he asked him why.

"You never stop thinkin', do you, James? Rosa Parsons is right. You're a thought machine."

If he hadn't known Dan was right, he might have felt attacked. But it was true. His mind never stopped, and he had this conscience that always seemed to be working overtime. "Can't be helped, I guess." He had to laugh at himself too.

He'd kept himself busy working, coaching the softball team, reading, being with his friends in the evening. But he felt restless for a whole month, wanting to get on with his life.

He woke up with the feeling and went to bed with it. Sometimes it felt like boredom, sometimes like irritation. Mixed in was a vapor-trail regret, at knowing he was leaving a family and close friends.

College, he kept repeating to himself. *New directions. Eventually some kind of career.* But for now something starkly different from what he woke up to every morning.

It was Wendy who sensed it most, the day he left for school, when she was in the driveway with him. "Can't wait to go, can you?" This as she tucked a laundry bag in the back seat for him.

He knew he should say all the things about missing her and the family, so he started to make something like a speech. But she cut him off, grinning.

"Stop," she said. "Just get in the car and try not to shriek when you leave the city limits! Love ya."

They had never been a family that expressed affection very physically, but on this occasion she gave him a hard hug and held on. He realized at that moment how close they were, he and Wendy, and his mom and him, and even his dad too, though everything was different with his father now.

The State University, Fall 1968

After his first long decade of fugitive seclusion, he risked venturing out once again, to the country's spaghetti freeways, neon light extravaganzas, fast-food havens, and "How're you today?" faces. Something drove him to emerge, morbid curiosity, he thought, probably no other rational explanation.

One morning on that foray he found himself atop a small hill overlooking a college campus, a pretty place in the old sense of campuses, spires poking out of ivy-shrouded structures, between which were idyllic sidewalks. Strolling on them was a new generation of students, ambling with carefree strides, and the sight of them stirred James' buried feelings.

Oh, what I could tell you! he caught himself saying, far from the young figures on the sunny sidewalks. *About college life in other times!*

There was this late-spring day years ago. Semester classes were over, not because the semester had ended but because the whole of the university had turned against a national government. Almost every school in the country did likewise, as desperate students gave up on education to show their anger. Their professors didn't care that they did because they were furious themselves. Unheard of, yes! But it happened.

Listen to me: The strolling you're doing now, that was impossible that day because National Guard troops and police were racing over green campus lawns, wolfing after young people like you, who'd been up half the night, setting bonfires and smashing things in rage at the nation's leader. It was a deadly game: taunt and react, the police as exhausted as the young people provoking them.

Imagine sirens going on all day long and most of the night. Continuous wailing sirens! Study with that din? Military trucks would hot-rod full throttle down the streets, and bystander students would shout "Pigs! Go home, Pigs!" The trucks would blast to a stop, and out their doors squirted helmeted personnel, chasing anyone standing nearby.

Listen! On my campus one poor devil, not a student but an insurance salesman, happened on that scene, on his usual walk to work. Why anyone would assume he was a student, no one could later explain (the guy in a pressed suit and carrying a smart briefcase), but somehow on that May morning that man found himself billy-clubbed and wobbly-kneed, falling toward the ground in disbelief before losing consciousness. The police were taking turns swinging, as though this ritual wasn't just their last resort but a privilege. Insane, insane. All of it because of an abstraction called government. I know, I know, it's not understandable. Nothing was comprehensible in those days.

Just remember this, on your way to your classes this morning. Just remember: This all happened in America! To people like you—students! Are you hearing me?

The ivy tower! Watching the young people traverse the campus pathways, he felt a deep jealousy. His generation had been cheated of the blithe freedom that was supposed to accompany college life. Back when he had been in school, history had draped a leaden cloak of disillusion over all of them.

At first, though, he recalled, it seemed like his years at the university would be no different than those of preceding generations.

"Yes, Mister Brandes? You're looking skeptical."

"Well, the president has enormous war-making powers now. I wonder how far one of our first presidents could have gone in their day."

His professor, a balding, skinny man, paused a moment before replying. "Class, what would the founding fathers have thought of the Gulf of Tonkin resolution? As the basis of the Vietnam War?"

A woman student to his left interrupted with heavy sarcasm: "But it's not a war officially. We just drop bombs into every rice paddy and send half a million guys over there."

"And spray lethal chemicals over a whole nation's food supply," someone else chimed in.

"Burn, baby, burn!"a third added. "Napalm for warmth on cool nights!"

Within no time the room was filled with grim humor, and Oates, who had a rich ironic sense, played on it.

"Okay," he said. "So the president can get away with things now? Things a Washington and Jefferson couldn't do? Yes?"

The sarcastic woman spoke again: "Sure, because he controls information. Johnson trumped up this phony attack, and no one but him could verify it."

"And nobody wanted to. Can't be a commie-lover."

"The truth was way on the other side of the world."

"The lies, you mean."

"Congress caved in."

Students were contributing so fast, Oates didn't know where to turn. He finally said to everyone and no one, "Sounds like the constitutional checks aren't as strong as they seem."

"Or Congress is unbalanced," somebody offered as a last quip. The comment brought a spatter of applause, and Mr. Oates announced they were out of time.

Out of the classroom, walking down the hill from the Social Sciences building, he felt the usual exhilaration from the class he had just been in. He loved ideas, loved putting them into contexts, testing the variables.

He'd never dreamed, back in high school, how intoxicating college could be. He not only thrived on it but craved it day after day, that previous year.

Partly, it was the honors program he'd been put into after the first semester, that made him so excited. The students he was in contact with seemed as turned on to learning as he was, and they never stopped challenging one another and their teachers. Discussions that started in classrooms trailed into restaurants, coffee houses, and bars. At least a couple of times a month he would find himself stressing a point, or listening to someone's else's, at one or two in the morning.

This year, his second, the newness of academic give-and-take had worn off somewhat, so he felt less stimulated. But he still thought he might just make academic life a career—get his Ph.D. and be a Professor Oates in his own right.

Along with the exhilaration he was feeling guilt, the squirmy discomfort he felt about once a week, which would come back to him when he thought about Harris Point.

If he were honest, he thought, he'd write his parents, especially his dad. *Dear folks*, the letter would begin, *I've done something I know you'll be unhappy with. Rather than hide what I'm saying, this is my way of letting you know that here on campus I actively work against the war in Vietnam. Twice a week I sit at a table in the student union where I distribute anti-war literature or ask people to sign petitions asking for U.S. withdrawal. I wanted you to know all this. I wanted to be open about everything.*

How noble of you, James, he told himself. *How hypocritical since you never actually write the letter, much less send it. You compose these thoughts, you muster these high sentiments, and then you let yourself be mired in cowardice.*

The year before, he'd formed his judgments about the war slowly. Immersed in his freshman studies during first semester, he pushed aside the issues. But during the second semester and during the summer, at home, the war screamed into his consciousness. He began to see it with a moral center and edges, and morality wasn't on the American side. Then, boom, came the North's TET Offensive in February with American cities falling under heavy attack, casualties heavy. So much for the invincible U.S!

At home legitimate politicians were finally challenging official war policy, as it became more bizarre. The war's point now seemed to be winning rather than winning for a reason.

A tide seemed to be rising against the Administration, but then the waters vanished, leaving the old gnat-at-your-ear paranoia. Had Martin Luther King and Robert Kennedy been gunned down by a super-patriot, right-wing cadre?

In early summer, at home in Harris Point, he was moody but in an oddly covert way. He was Mister Bland in front of his parents and Mister Sulk in his room. He avoided being in the living room with his father, where the TV had the latest grim stories, but he took the imaged body counts upstairs, in his doubt-plagued head. Even in August, with the outrages of the Democratic convention, he kept up the facade of unbothered nice guy.

Only Wendy seemed to catch on, but she let him be, which he was thankful for. "You okay?" she asked one morning, and he told her he just needed time to think. But she looked worried, and probably she had good reason to. Living the two separate lives in one body hadn't been healthy. Yet he couldn't explain why he let it go on.

Nearing the apartment he shared with Frank, a Biology major, he saw the woman he'd been in class with, the one who'd started the jeering tide late in the hour. She waved and came across the street.

"I'm Beth," she said, shaking his hand.

"With the great sense of humor, obviously."

"Sometimes maybe. Thanks."

He found out she lived only a block from him, on the third floor of a frame house like the one he was in. When she talked she tilted off center, her left hip out, as though sizing someone up. She had loose auburn hair and pale green eyes.

"Like to get together sometime?" he found himself asking. After his high school experience with Heather, he'd been a slow-goer with women the previous year, but this one seemed to invite openness.

"Love to. But I'll warn you, I talk a lot."

"Something wrong with that?"

"Coffee after class on Wednesday then."

As she strolled away, he called after her: "I'm a good listener! Really."

"I know," he heard. "I've watched you."

At his apartment he picked up the mail from the kitchen counter. One item was a letter from his senator, and he opened it with not much expectation. People in Washington seemed paralyzed with inertia.

Oct. 1, 1968

Dear Mr. Brandes:

Thank you for your recent letter about our Vietnam involvement.

I am now opposed to our present level of engagement. I believe our military miscalculated how long the war would take, and how strong our allies, the South Vietnamese, are.

Recent estimates show that we now spend thirteen million dollars an hour on this war, this for a country the size of Washington state. This seems an intolerable waste of money.

A number of us in the U.S. Senate are waiting for the proper time to press for changes in our defense policy. Right now we don't wish to propose specific legislation, but we are ready to act decisively if the war effort weakens further.

Sincerely,

He tossed the letter into the wastebasket, as he repeated its key phrase: *Ready to act decisively if.* "If!" he jeered to the empty room, "If, if, if! Thank you, Senator, for your courage, your integrity, your shining example!"

He heard his own voice and was frightened by its harshness, which was there more insistently since the start of the school year.

The bitterness had begun to creep in, the previous fall, when more and more students like him had questioned the U.S.'s commitment in Asia. Then, in December, President Johnson appeared on television. His president but a sad goon at best! "We're going to win!" he said repeatedly, as though his emphasizing forefinger was something to stab with. His commander in the field, General Westmoreland, was full of confidence now.

Bitter January. The president escalated the war, he recalled. Troop numbers went up as student faith in government slid downward. The north launched the TET offensive, squashing the military's optimism.

Campus life changed. Students in his dorm were drinking more, and many were using LSD as well as pot. For the disillusioned, not attending classes was becoming almost chic.

All over the campus billboards were beginning to fill with anti-war literature. Average guys were letting their hair grow long as a protest against the established order. Everybody was throwing fashionable clothing into closets and heading for the army-surplus stores, to buy military jackets. Mocking the generals! it was called.

He found many things amusing, as the pluckiness of the protesters kept everybody as upbeat as they could be. But oh, the stupidity, he thought, the silly equations of the political left, which had taken to printing bumper stickers saying DON'T TRUST ANYONE OVER THIRTY. Everything they opposed was tagged as "The Establishment."

He was just as amazed at the counter-literature he saw, the mindless, blind patriotism of the political right's AMERICA: LOVE IT OR LEAVE IT sloganeering.

February! Gloomy. Weirdly, he and his fellow students finally found some hope. A senator, Eugene McCarthy, decided to challenge the president in the presidential primaries, just on the issue of Vietnam.

On primary election day, early March—that wonderful night!—McCarthy won.

In the large lounge of the student union, more and more students came in as the newscast confirmed McCarthy's upset. Soon some two hundred of them were crowded together, happier than they'd been in months.

The vote announcement was a tonic for opinions, he remembered. A student close to the TV was saying McCarthy could take other primaries, even beat Johnson. Someone else argued that wouldn't happen, but Robert Kennedy, the assassinated president's brother, could join the race and actually win.

Outside the lounge that night, large snowflakes were falling, slapping like an ovation against the huge plate glass window. Was nature confirming a change of heart in the country? Inside they felt some optimism at long last.

Optimism. Where was it now? He lay down on the couch, his memory-stream continuing despite his efforts to shut it down. He tried to nap but couldn't. Ate, tried to study, couldn't. He went to bed but was up at two. Frank found him prowling the kitchen and asked if he was okay.

"Just dealing with a mind boiling over," he answered.

"Well at least you're not turning into a dope-head." Frank's hand was absent-mindedly trying to comb his disordered black hair.

No, he wasn't, but was memory a bad trip too?

Kennedy had entered the race in a matter of weeks and was praised as a savior of the party or jeered as a political opportunist riding the coat-tails of the courageous McCarthy. But there was a vague feeling that the two candidates could join forces at some time to make a change. Either they could win enough primaries to force Johnson out of his party's nomination, or they could embarrass the president so much, he'd start withdrawing troops soon.

Against this thinking came Frank's nay-saying: Johnson was a political pro who would rally his forces, drum out the opposition, and escalate the war even further, even though more and more students were seeing LBJ as a demagogue. He'd been burned in effigy on campus at least once.

James stirred the herbal tea he'd made. Two-thirty now, and he struggled to link the memories into a chronology. But the thoughts concentrated in a single face.

Johnson! His response came only weeks later, as pollsters were showing him headed for defeat in coming primaries. James was in a local hangout, Headwaters, watching the president on the corner TV, and the man looked haggard, eyes glazed over, cataracted. His wire-rimmed glasses sat heavily on his nose, and when he leaned forward, it looked as though his neck ached.

He and his fellow bar-goers braced for more bad news, and they got it, in the announcement of additional troops being sent. But then the president announced a peace initiative, a halt in the bombing in return for negotiations with Hanoi.

There was strong mixed reaction. At a table to his left some roused students were shouting "Hypocrite!" and "More troops in the name of peace! Bullshit!" But a few people, James included, saw a crack in the war policy for the first time.

Could they afford to ease up on their efforts? Go back to being just students again?

Then Johnson took them all by surprise, announcing he wasn't going to be running again. He was dropping out of the upcoming presidential race.

For a moment no one grasped the meaning of Johnson's words, but then Headwaters exploded with cheering, whistling, and clapping. Someone shouted: "All the way with LBJ! Tune in, drop out!" And the room boomed with howling, as though it were an autumn Saturday, and some favorite home-team back was just scoring a winning touchdown.

He left the bar that night, long months before, bouncy in his walk. They'd gotten rid of LBJ, and it was only a matter of time for the war to be ended. All over campus students were celebrating.

He caught Beth after class and said he'd meet her later at Warren's Restaurant since he had something to do that would take ten minutes. Then he went to Oates' office, knowing he'd be there.

Oates was happy to see him, asking him to sit, inquiring if something wasn't clear in class."No, I'm here on another matter."

He drew out the petition, explaining its purpose. Students wanted faculty to drop research funded by the military for the war. "Just doing what you've suggested," he added, "exercising my right as an individual to petition."

"And this is going to—?"

"The Board of Regents."

"Ah!" The monosyllable had ambiguous weight, as Oates read the document, noted the names of some of his colleagues, but then let the petition rest inertly on his desk. He shifted elaborately in his chair.

"I suppose you'll be surprised when I say I can't sign this."

"I certainly will. Why not?"

Oates went into a lengthy dissertation about the fragility of universities, the necessity of one department not antagonizing another, the importance of the right timing as an element of viable civil protest. As he talked, his professor almost seemed to be playing some elaborate ruse. Could this be yet another bit of irony by one of its masters? Yet he knew that wasn't true.

"When exactly would be the right time for you to sign?" he cut in.

Oates meditated. "Maybe when the chairman of the department signs on."

"You do understand, the university is collaborating in military operations."

"Unfortunately, no university's research is ever totally untainted."

"But you're against the war."

"Absolutely."

He didn't know whether to say what was on his mind, but he went ahead: "Unless the university can keep making money from it?"

Oates was becoming uncomfortable. "I don't know that I'd quite put it that way. Incidentally, I've been meaning to ask if you need a grad school recommendation."

"I'm only a sophomore," he replied, getting to his feet and taking the petition back. "Thanks for your time."

"You're welcome, Mister Brandes. Always good talking to you." Oates wiped away the small dots of sweat on his upper lip, as his student turned and left.

Beth didn't believe it any more than he did at first, though his frustration was stronger. "He seems so liberal," she said. "Did you go alone?"

"Yes, why?"

"Better if you go in a group, three or four of you. Give me the petition. Some of us will pay him a visit in a day or two."

"Sounds like you've done this before."

She told him that her parents were political activists, people who'd often taken her with, in her childhood, when they worked neighborhoods for various causes.

She was quick-witted and sometimes sharp-tongued, but then she had an engaging way, too, of referring to herself in the third person, making jokes on herself. "Beth Stephens strikes again,"she jibed at herself, as she described a social gaffe she'd let fly a week before.

She was an English major with a gift for words, she said, and a talent for talking her way into trouble. She was from a Chicago suburb, loved nice cars, hated the new James Bond, was thinking of a California trip the coming summer, was allergic to cats but only the short-hairs, pigged out on potato chips, always had trouble inhaling at pot parties, had been on a high school swim team but almost detested sports now.

"And I warned you that I talked a lot, didn't I? But you didn't believe me."

"Actually...."

"But you do now."

"Yes." He found himself a little bewildered, as well as amused.

"It's okay," she said, putting her hand on his momentarily. "After ten at night my voice gives out, and I become catatonic. You'll see, James."

"I'll take your word for it," he said. He had the feeling he'd just had a first meeting with someone who would be a life-long friend.

The next night he was studying for a Chem 202 quiz, when the phone rang, and Frank told him it was Humphrey headquarters calling. Organizers wanted him to distribute some campaign literature on campus.

Though he'd studied the vice-president's record and liked most of it, the man was still refusing to turn his back on Johnson and the war. But any day now, the caller said, Humphrey's announcement would come. He told the caller that when it did, he'd do some work for the campaign.

After the call he tried to study but couldn't. In the middle of a formula he was working through, his mind went raggedly back in time again, to the political convulsions of the previous spring.

McCarthy! After knocking off LBJ, his constituency began to shift to Kennedy, who had a better chance of winning his party's nomination, insiders thought.

Humphrey! The vice-president had announced his own campaign and was doing well, with one hitch. Before the war he'd been well thought of by students, but he was still refusing to renounce Vietnam.

Spring. April. Martin Luther King snipered away in Memphis, another in the long line of murdered black activists.

Memories of JFK's killing came back: despair as a facet of daily life, disbelief as part of one's waking hours. Plus, the renewed suspicion that any anti-war figure was doomed. James remembered being in a favorite restaurant, telling friends he felt cornered at times, when no one whatsoever was watching. The friends, it turned out, were having similar moments.

Thankfully, semester exams re-focused everyone and steadied their emotions. Wonderful weather was ahead, and a full summer. Politically Robert Kennedy was gaining ground by the day.

Till Kennedy went, in early June, the hand-gun bullet in his brain, dead like his brother, a week later. Was there any grief left in the emotional bank? *It can't get worse than this,* James told himself.

No, no worse–but almost as bad as. The Democratic convention! Those August days! That profanity of democratic exercise. No chance for anyone on their side to win the nomination. Humphrey weaseling, still refusing to renounce. Where was the courage the man had shown in the early civil rights era? He'd been a champion of right causes.

In the streets outside the convention there was the raw, defiant brutality by the chief defenders of the law.

Nixon! The One! The Republican answer! Smug. Saying he had a plan to end the war and smoothly asserting he couldn't discuss it because it would give aid to the enemy.

Back on campus, now, this fall, the whole student body knew that Nixon was bluffing, his dishonesty a campus joke. But the polls were showing that the ruse was working elsewhere. He was probably going to win the election.

Everyone was feeling helpless again, faced with a choice between Humphrey, who might find courage again but might not, and Nixon, the one! the obvious liar.

Trying to refocus on his chemistry textbook, he recalled the name his philosophy instructor had used, last semester, to describe what they'd all been feeling: existential despair, the choice of having no choice.

It wasn't any easier dealing with the feeling, he thought, if you had a label for it. The feeling was still there.

He liked her more and more. One afternoon they took a long walk to a city park, and there she regaled him with a history of her relationships with guys in her high school. She'd agreed to go to a movie that night with somebody and was worried that history was going to repeat itself.

She called them the three musketeers: Don, Dave, and Duh, otherwise known as Aaron.

Don, she said, was the son of her parents' friends, so there was a family connection that led her to thinking he'd be someone to know better. But on their second night out alone, Don became a grope fiend, as she put it, an outer-space alien in disguise, with digital apparatus that defied science. She worked up a sweat fending him off, and when she told her mother about him, her mom said she'd always suspected as much, which led her into the first and only real fight she ever had with her mother.

Dave was the one with the sports car. She had this uncle who had a sports car, and he was wonderful, so she assumed all sports car owners were wonderful, but Dave came from a family so busy with their professional advancement that they had a meaningful talk with their children exactly once a year. That was on Thanksgiving, two hours before turkey time, with five children battling their parents' attenuated listening skills because Mom and Dad went from tall bloody-marys at brunch to dinner martinis mid-afternoon. Dave sorely needed a confidant, and she became his counselor and psychiatrist for six months, after which she told him that either she was entitled to professional fees or total silence on their next three times out. Dave did the clever thing, thanked her, dropped her, and spent the next year at a counseling clinic.

Duh, Aaron, was the rebound of Dave. She welcomed his mute manner until she discovered he had nothing to say. At first she thought he was sensitive, but then she intuited he was only brain-cell-deprived. His range of discussion on any subject lasted two sentences, and finally her best friend had to tell her the truth, that if Aaron had anything upstairs, the windows were wide open and a tornado was coming down the road. Luckily, when she decided to rid herself of him, he didn't even recognize she was putting time, place, and emotions between them.

"Got it!"she said. "The man signed on." She came up to him at the table in the student union lounge where he was sitting. She was crowing a little.

"Good for you. How'd you do it?"

"We just sat there and demolished his arguments. After we sucked up to him of course. All these guys are egotists, face it."

"Cynic. I don't think of Oates that way."

"Blind idealism, Jamesie boy!"she joked. "Anyway, that makes forty faculty names on the petition, right?"

"Forty-two. We're making headway."

"But only four are on the Faculty Senate, out of sixteen, and that's who the regents listen to." Her realism came back, along with a dejected look. "Maybe the military will go for a higher profile on what they're doing, let out something they shouldn't. So far they've been our best help." She added grimly: "Some friends we've got!"

The next morning, after his Abnormal Psych class, he was working the tables distributing information about the war.

He wasn't sure how he'd become a regular volunteer, nor that he considered himself a hard-core war protester. He'd just drifted into this activity, he liked his co-volunteers, and it seemed natural for him to be where he was a couple of hours a week, at the student union.

Most of the time one or two students would drop by every hour, to pick up what new leaflet was available that day. Or they'd just stop by to chat.

This morning he had to deal with a sad case, a freckled face student from Missouri, who let his grades slip and was being called up by his draft board. He was from a rural area, and the board didn't have many guys in the draft pool, so he was a prime target for possible induction.

In a state of confusion the guy had enlisted, but now he regretted it.

Feeling helpless himself, he gave him the name and phone number of a lawyer in town, a Quaker, who was giving free legal advice to war resistors and others. The student thanked him warmly and left.

Sitting there, he was reminded of the trip his family had taken to campus, prior to his enrolling. His father had made that scene about lazy draft dodgers giving out literature, and his mother reassured his dad: James had his head on his shoulders and would have nothing to do with such an activity.

Yet here he was, right in the middle of it.

Was that why he felt guilty? Because of the deception? Or because he was going contrary to all his hometown values about the military? Probably his feelings came more from the former than the latter, but their source didn't matter. For the first time, close to his visit to Harris Point, he understood that he and his dad would clash sometime over his beliefs. And he would wound his father deeply.

"Why me?"she complained. "I seem to attract them! Damn!"

He offered her his sympathy, but he told her the whole thing did seem a bit funny.

"I know, but you didn't have to live through it."

Beth had gotten to know a good looking guy a week before, in the student union. He'd invited her to a weekend outing with friends on a farm owned by the guy's acquaintances, but once there she discovered that the outing group was heavily into nature mysticism.

They all headed out to a hillside to absorb the autumn colors. "You know what the word *absorb* means, James?" Her question had a mix of high energy disbelief and anger.

"Obviously not."

"Looking, staring, staring, seeing. Those idiots and I on the hill, and the trees opposite."

"There's nothing wrong with that. The colors must be at their peak."

"Looking, staring, looking some more."

"How long?" He was beginning to sense what she had gone through.

"Two hours, in one place. We were supposed to commune! With the maples, the oaks, even the ones the woodpeckers had beaked to death!"

"Was there dope involved?"

"Not a bit! Just mindless boredom. After the first ten minutes Nathan took me aside to tell me there's a little rule they have: no talking."

"Aha! Now we're down to the nitty-gritty!"

Beth barely paused for breath. "Seems talking diminishes the experience. 'How about sleep, Nathan?' I said. 'What if I drop off?' and he tells me it might be okay, but it might be insulting to the trees."

"What?"

"If we've established a relationship! he said."

"Good god."

"Why?" she repeated. "Why me? Got a wiggy brain? A mental problem? Sign up for a date with Beth? Socially dysfunctional? Get in line!"

"It'll be all right," he reassured her, trying to hold in his amusement.

They ran into Frank, wolfing a burger and fries at Warren's, and he motioned them over to his table. Between bites his face showed a cynical amusement.

"Sit," he ordered them. "I've got some news for you, a little surprise. You know that guy Creighton, who works the literature tables with you once in a while?"

"Creighton Wallace, yeah."

Frank leaned his square chest closer to them, lowering his voice: "A government spy."

"What?" He and Beth were echoing each other's disbelief.

"Some of the March-on-Washington gang figured it out. He's supposedly from this small Illinois town, but when we called the only Wallace there, there was no one who'd ever heard of a Creighton Wallace. He's an art major too, but somebody went to the Art Department, posed as him, and asked for a transcript of his last semester's grades."

"Which didn't exist," Beth finished for him, guessing right.

Frank smiled ruefully. "Standard protester clothing—faded jeans, flannel shirt, army jacket. Creighton's got all of it, including the boots. But the boots are always spit-shined. Military mentality. Are we dumb or dumb, that we didn't notice?"

"So who's going to confront him?"

"We're not, James. We're going to use him—feed him false information if we need to.

"God, we've gotten down to cat and mouse now," Beth lamented.

He read his sister's letter when he got home. It made him nervous again, forcing him to confront once more his thoughts from earlier in the day.

Dear James,

Since you're going to be home next week, I wanted to drop you a note about the home scene here.

Dad's been real sulky and quiet around here for months. He comes home and turns on the TV, trying to find out as much news as can about the Vietnam War. He doesn't joke like he used to, and he doesn't talk a lot.

I think all this started about winter, when that TET Offensive thing came on TV. (That was the right name for it, wasn't it?). Dad was just shocked that those troops from the north could make our own look so helpless. He thought the war was going to end any day.

Anyway, he's a TV vegetable now, but the problem is, the war news isn't good when he wants it to be. Dad's also stopped going to church since he still thinks Pastor Allen is sympathetic to the anti-war people, which is totally ridiculous as you know. Poor Pastor Allen! Mom resents Dad thinking this way, but she can't talk to Dad about it, and she feels embarrassed too, at his not being in the pew next to us on Sundays. Last Sunday as she was leaving the house for church she even shouted at him for being a lazy heathan (sp?).

Anyway, I'd like to ask you not to mention the war at Thanksgiving. Let's just have a good old time like we always do, okay?

I've narrowed my college list to three. Can you believe I'll be a Harris Point grad next June? Wow!

I'm learning French furiously. My teacher is an exchange teacher from Rouen, and he's luscious looking. Tell you more about him and everything else when you're here.

"Au revoir,"

Wendy

"Trouble in River City," he said. "Thanksgiving isn't going to be much fun."

Beth had gone to get them two coffees, which she now set in front of them. By now their after-class ritual was so established that they knew exactly how many sugar cubes the other took, how much stirring was done, and whether the cup was nursed for ten or twenty minutes, depending on what circumstances.

"So what's up in the Brandes household? Snoopy Beth wants to know."

"My dad's in this huge funk about the war apparently. My sister says he seems obsessed by all the war news on TV."

"Like father, like son," Beth said, "for different reasons."

"Hey, I've been better lately. I turn off the tube now, a lot of times, for my own sanity."

"Not a bad idea."

They were quiet a minute, then they both started talking at once: "Did you see—?" "God, last night there was—"

He let her go first.

"This U.S. colonel last night, on camera, mind you, right there, saying it with a straight face!"

"'We had to destroy—'"

She blurted him into cooperative silence. "Right: '—We had to destroy the village to save it.'"

"You saw it too!"

"Couldn't believe it! Christ! Do they teach that doublespeak at officer candidate school?"

"You missed some of it then," Beth said. "The guy was a West Pointer."

"You're joking."

"The nation's finest, four years of college at your patriotic taxpayer's expense, Brandes—a lean, mean, idiotic machine!"

"Destroy a village to save it," he repeated.

They lapsed into a momentary mood, a feeling that had become familiar all over campus: black humor wearing off into misery. The video image of the officer talking against the backdrop of the smoldering Vietnam village—that was in their heads now too.

Nor was it just a question of images. The whole illogic of the war came to them over and over. Frank, two weeks before, had stumbled onto yet another example of it, in a bar with friends. The friends had bumped into other friends, who had a Vietnamese woman in their group, about twenty-four, whose family had recently immigrated to the U.S. Stunningly fluent in English, at some point in the evening she related her previous role in South Vietnam, that of translator in the office of the general staff of U.S. forces. Then she explained one of the policies she had to follow.

Frank had to ask her again what she was saying, since he couldn't really grasp the woman's point. He thought he'd had one too many beers.

"No, it's true," she reiterated.

"Wait. The general staff had you sign a paper saying you wouldn't understand the words you were translating? You could only change them from one language to another?"

The woman nodded as Frank tried again: No, what the officers must have meant, he offered, was that the translators were forbidden to understand *the context* of what they were translating. Right?

"No, the words themselves," the woman said.

"How could you translate if you didn't understand the words?"

"You can't,"the woman said, shrugging her petite shoulders.

"That's ridiculous!"

"Yes." Then the woman explained how she and some of the other translators went to their superiors to say that the policy defied logic. "It didn't matter to them," she told Frank. "They just told us to sign the paper anyway, so we did."

Two days after Nixon's election, the weather was unusually warm, temperature in the sixties, so he and Beth went to sit on the terrace of the student union, overlooking the lakefront. Neither of them had been surprised at the vote outcome, and they were half-heartedly trying to convince themselves that the new president wouldn't be the die-hard Cold War warrior he'd once been. It was easier not to think about the politics at all and watch the ducks on the water, to think about the natural cycle of seasons turning. There was comfort in knowing that a segment of life would continue as always, predictably.

He'd voted for Humphrey—the lesser of two evils—as he put it, while Beth left the presidency slot untouched. And when he asked her why, after class the previous day, she'd simply held her nose, saying "Phew!" in that sardonic manner she often used with artful effect.

He knew Beth well enough to know she had reasons for not supporting Humphrey, so he let her be then. Now, though, as they watched two mallards scrap for territory ten yards from shore, he prodded her.

Beth was surprisingly dismissive about his question, so he asked again, in a different way. This time she made a joking remark just as evasive, so he asked once more, going back to his original wording. But Beth blank-faced him.

After he looked at her for a couple of long seconds, trying to figure out what she was up to, she finally blurted out, "I'm embarrassed about this, James."

Now he was really in the dark, but he forged on, saying that voting for any reason was okay.

Beth confronted him: "You know that's not true. You and I, and most of our friends, we detest people who walk into those booths and pull levers because Congressman Jerk once played for the New York Jets or because the price of tires went up the day before the election."

"Right, I guess. But how does that relate to you?"

Suddenly a look of mortification came onto her face. "I'm one of those detestables."

"Oh, come on!"

"No, I acted for the silliest reason, based on something that happened on the way to the polls. I passed that woman Fetal, all balled up at a bus stop."

Fetal was a campus character, a former grad student named Charlene, who'd been normal until the previous summer, when she'd gone with friends to Chicago, to demonstrate at the Democratic convention. Savagely mauled there by the city's police, she returned to the campus this fall appearing normal. But then she started acting strange, curling herself into a wombic ball, in the library stacks, in store entryways, and at concession stands outside the football stadium. She'd stay like that for an hour, mute to helpful passers-by, and then get up and leave.

Mental health agencies tried to help her, but Fetal resisted aid, moving out of her dorm room and maybe taking up residence on the street, though no one knew that for sure. Local high school kids were making pilgrimages to campus on weekends to see if they could see her, and rumors were spreading about a book of poetry Fetal had supposedly written, entitled "Spleen Scream."

"So tell me the connection between Fetal and your voting." James was still in the dark.

"Oh, it's so simple,"Beth said, "So damned stupid! I passed her on the way to vote, and when I got in the booth, she was still in my head. I wanted to vote for Humphrey, but then I left him hang there. I didn't vote at all. I was paying back the Democratic party for what they did to that half-crazy woman. What an idiotic thing to do!"

He started to say something like it wasn't crazy at all, although he didn't believe it, but she cut him off impatiently: "Don't make this worse, James!" She made him promise never to tell anyone what she'd done.

They ate, they talked, they told each other about the things in their daily lives. There was turkey, mashed potatoes, pumpkin pie. Smiles, jokes, stories of past family adventures—a real Norman Rockwell painting, he told Beth when he came back to campus. Wendy was delighted the way things went, and his dad had seemed more relaxed than in months. His mother took great pride in her holiday meal.

The only time they got close to the taboo subject came when his father told him the news about Howard. He was going to have to leave college because Norm, his father, could no longer support himself. "Can you believe it?" his mother said. "After all they've been through, and now Norm Parker has Parkinson's Disease!"

"He'll make a good soldier," his dad said.

"Pardon?" James stopped his chewing.

His mother and Wendy were exchanging stricken looks. Vietnam was just off-stage.

"Howard's joining the service after this semester," his dad said matter-of-factly. "Janine, this was a lovely meal, one of the best you've ever done." He made an elaborate ritual of kissing her on the cheek, and she beamed in his recognition. When he left the table, though, a moment later, both his mother and sister were still tense.

Next morning he was on his way to see Howard but had to stop for gas. At the pump he ran into Rosa, his old high school friend, who became instantly excited.

She insisted he follow her, and when he wanted to know where, she wouldn't tell him. She just said it wouldn't take long.

They drove up, in separate cars, to a small house a mile from the gas station. When they got out she was radiant, as she made a sweeping gesture toward the structure behind her.

"What do you think, James?"

"Your bungalow? Your family finally got it?" He was pleased for her, hugging her.

"That new civil rights law about housing—that did it!" she said. "Uncle Sam came through."

She brought him inside to meet her family, her parents and two small sisters. They were people easy to get to know, and he wished he could stay longer.

On the way out of the house, they encountered Rosa's brother coming in, on his crutches. They all chatted briefly, and then he got in his car. As James saw Gerald awkwardly maneuvering through the front door of the house, he recalled the Fourth of July, seventeen months previous, when he'd seen this man as the object of the town's celebration. Now the parade was over, and the daily grimace of a handicapped walk was the reality. And in twenty years, when the war was only a faint breeze of a memory, would anyone know what he represented? Too, as the war was being seen more and more in a bad light, veterans were coming home less as heroes. Did Gerald wake in the middle of the night, anger crying through his chest all the way down to his clenched fists?

Well at least the Parsons had gotten their house, they and other blacks like them, he thought.

But what a grim exchange, he reminded himself: The Lord giveth bungalows, the Lord taketh away legs.

A half hour later he and Howard were in a bar, and he was asking if Howard's decision was final. His old friend told him he didn't have much choice. What with working to keep the family going, he'd dropped most of his classes, which got him drafted. In one way, though, it wasn't such a bad solution. He wasn't enjoying being at home, with his dad more and more house-bound irritated, more and more angry, even though his mom was a good amateur nurse.

"Well, this way you'll have your steady army income and won't have to feel bad about being away."

"And there'll be scholarships the army gives me, when I get out."

He thought about saying how sad he was that everything had worked out badly for Howard, but he knew he didn't have to. His face was showing how he felt, and they'd been friends a long time, without a need to say the obvious.

"What about Vietnam?" He knew they'd have to discuss the subject eventually, so he raised it now.

"I'm going to try to get to Germany instead," Howard said. "But who knows...?"

"Too bad you couldn't have had Randy's money."

Howard didn't respond, draining his glass. After a long moment he said: "I hear he may be transferring out of that small school he's at. He's bored, I gather."

"Real fine reason," James sneered. "Want another tap?"

"Why not?" Howard said. Suddenly, though, he looked as though his mind was already away, a thousand miles from Harris Point. He looked frail as well as frightened.

"So he didn't find out about your anti-draft work?"

"I didn't want him to, remember. But then I really felt on the edge of it."

They were heading for the library to study, and he was telling Beth more about Thanksgiving back home.

"It's not right, James. You ought to tell him."

"But Wendy told me his health really isn't very good now."

"That's your answer then: You shouldn't say anything. I guess."

"And go on being a hypocrite?"

"Better that than sending your dad into a heart attack or something. He must have seen some heavy combat in Korea, to feel this strongly. Yes?"

"Just the opposite. He was never in any actual battle."

"Maybe that explains why he wants it so badly for you," Beth said, leaning into his shoulder for a moment in a gesture of closeness.

"I've thought of that. I've given up trying to figure it all out since I'm not sure it's all based in any one thing. Sure is frustrating though."

"We can talk about it more,"she told him, "if you want to. It looks like bearing guilt is all you can do for now. Unless you tell your mom to tell your dad."

"I couldn't do that to her. It'd be cowardly."

Beth conceded his point, but then she reflected: "I bet she knows, though, don't you think?"

He'd never thought of this before, and he pondered the possibility, noting that Beth always had good antennae about people. "I'm not sure," he told her. "She hides the secret well if she does know."

"Self-protection,"Beth suggested. "Good for her."

His dear friend Beth. He was reminded of her insights and temperament the next weekend, at a semester-end party. Nursing a beer in the kitchen doorway of the apartment below his and Frank's, he watched with amusement as Frank, across the living room, tried to extricate himself from conversation with a spindly blond. The woman's voice was rising to a shrill pipe that even dominated the loud stereo. She had her face close to Frank's, riveting his eye contact, and his roommate was tilting backwards, like a dental patient being drilled.

Frank finally worked himself free and came over. "Whew. More of the latest we talked about, people screaming rather than talking. I feel rescued."

"The new campus chic," James agreed. "Big political points for it these days. Too bad, buddy." They both sipped a minute, surveying their fellow party-goers. Then he said, "Why don't you try that one on the floor at the end of the sofa? She looks mild enough."

"You first," Frank came back. "Find out if she bites."

They could joke about such things now, at the party, but they'd had a long talk recently about shouting as a new talking style on campus. Both from civil households, they flinched at the chainsaw rasp of so many campus radicals.

"Say you're shrill all the time, for shock," Frank pointed out. "That goes only so far. Sooner or later you'll just come off as a whiney brat."

Frank also relished describing something he called radical sincerity, after he saw a confrontation between a campus dean and a hyperventilating male activist. On-camera, the activist flung insult after insult at the dean; cameras off, the radical tried to shake hands with him before heading to a new TV event.

"Weird way to win friends and influence people,"his roommate said wryly. "Like, 'How 'bout if we get together for chit-chat, you and me, after I kick you in the kidneys?'"

The University and Harris Point, Christmas 1968–June 1969

Back home in Harris Point at Christmas break, he had trouble getting his father's car started in the cold, black light of the January morning, so he thought he'd be late getting to the bus depot. But when he got there he saw everyone milling about. Working men in old jackets stood by their wives in pin curls and bandanas while their sons smoked or fidgeted with duffel bags, swinging them slightly against their sides. It was too early for anyone to talk much. In one corner of the waiting room, over near the rows of lockers, the man who ran the newsstand mechanically snipped the wires on the morning's bundled papers.

He spotted Howard and his folks sitting on one of the old wooden benches. At their feet was a small puddle of water the three of them had made with the slush dripping from their shoes. Their backs to him, he walked over and said hello.

"James!" Howard's mother had a high-pitched, thin voice that carried even more in this quiet hour of the morning in the tiled waiting room. "What a nice surprise!"

He shook hands with Howard's father, whose right hand trembled visibly, and winked to Howard, who was starting a yawn. "I thought I'd come see you off. I didn't sleep that well last night anyway."

Howard gaped through the last of his yawn and broke into a nervous laugh. "I guess I didn't either," he said. He looked apprehensive, an unprotected rabbit in a bare field.

"You probably won't get much sleep in the next weeks either," he said, regretting it immediately. Why remind his friend of the misery he would be going through in basic training?

They talked on and off until a uniformed man came into the room and started calling out roster names. Howard told him Jennifer had chosen not to see him off. She'd embarrass him with her tears, she said, which he understood in one way.

The roll went rapidly. As they got nearer his place in the alphabet, Howard looked more and more tentative, and when his voice was called, he squeaked out a weak reply.

The four of them moved outside, where the air stung, toward the bus. Before getting on, Howard kissed his mother, who was crying, and hugged his father, who was comforting his wife. At the last second father and son faced each other.

"Don't take any chances," Norm Parker said, shaking—from Parkinson's or fear, James wondered.

"I won't, Dad." He turned: "James, thanks for coming. It means a lot." Then he lifted his heavy body into the tall steps of the silver metallic Greyhound.

Through the tinted green glass they could barely see him. But they waved bravely as the bus edged out of the parking lot. Afterwards the diesel smell of its engine hung in his nostrils, even in the sub-zero temperatures. He felt awake now and nauseous. His friend would be safe, wouldn't he, in Germany or somewhere else besides Vietnam, where he could get himself stationed?

They spent three long days together, unplanned, in early February, when she caught severe flu. They were at his and Frank's place listening to music, near midnight, when Beth started to feel nauseous. She told him she was going to go home, but then she was so woozy she nearly fainted getting her coat on, and by then, too, she was a body of shivers. He headed her toward his bed and got her under the covers, thinking that whatever it was would pass by morning.

By noon the next day, having spent the night vomiting, she was beyond going home to her apartment. He'd taken up residence on the living room couch, when he could sleep. But he was up almost as frequently as she was, putting compresses on her forehead, keeping a steady supply of aspirin going, to fight her fever.

It broke on the third day, and she gave way to extended sleep. That afternoon he was sitting on the edge of the bed, and he couldn't bear more dozing on the lumpy couch, so he edged down beside her for a second, fighting his own fatigue. He woke three hours later, the two of them spooned together in exhaustion recovery.

"If that was your idea of seduction," he heard her say wearily into his ear, "then you're confusing snoring and foreplay."

"You're better," he said happily. "Thank god."

"You're a wonderful nurse," she said. "Do you have the strength to go to Warren's and get me some vegetable soup?"

When he came back, she was propped against the pillow, which was against the wall. After she ate she asked him for a mirror, and when she looked at herself in it, she peeped out an exclamation of disgust and horror: "Jesus, James, I look terrible. Really. My hair looks like hell."

"It doesn't matter," he soothed.

"It does. This is a woman thing you wouldn't understand."

She wanted to take a bath, so he ran the water for her, but by the time he came to tell her everything was ready, she'd fallen asleep again. Her hair had fallen over her cheek, and he brushed aside some of its auburn strands. It was the first time he'd really studied her face when she wasn't in the midst of conversation. He thought, for a second anyway, that she was pretty. Why hadn't he noticed before?

They'd been given a reprieve.

The new president, Nixon, was forming his cabinet in the early months of the year, letting the war go on without much change. Troop withdrawals, though small, had begun.

While everyone waited to see what would happen nationally, he and his fellow students could study again, and he savored the hours in the library he'd given up the previous fall. He still worked the anti-war literature tables in the student union, but less frequently.

The academic routine steadied him and brought him back to his intellectual self. In late January protest groups broke into draft board offices in three cities, burning records. A week afterwards, a group of Catholic activists chained themselves to a weapons plant gate and were being charged with treason. But he let the news reports of the events stay on television, not in his mind.

The day the last big snow of the season fell, he finished an exam and came right home, stomping the wet white stuff off on the stairway.

When he got to the landing he was surprised to find the door unlocked. And Beth was on the couch, reading a magazine.

"How was it?"she asked brightly.

"Not bad, not bad at all."

"And you're wondering what I'm doing here?"

"Yes. Not that I mind."

"Frank and I arranged this, and don't worry, I'm not going to come down with flu again. You're really going to like this."

"Like what? I don't understand."

"I know. Take off your coat." She got up to go to the kitchen and came back carrying two glasses of wine.

He was still confused but willing to let her continue whatever it was that was going on. In his mind, too, was a sentence that he been running through his mind lately, for her: "What would you think about our going out, not as friends, but...well, you know?" He didn't want to ruin a friendship, but he had different kind of feelings toward her recently.

She had him sit down. They chatted until they'd finished their drinks.

"Now," she said, "we need to clear the air about something."

"Such as?"

"Our attraction for each other. This is Valentine's Day after all."

"But we've never gone out, formally. I mean I'd love to."

"We spend gobs of time together and like each other a lot. Admit it."

He laughed. She'd caught him. "True, Beth. Always right, aren't you?"

"And you want me."

"What?"

"You want me. Don't be bashful about this."

"You're audacious. We've never even kissed!"

"Oh, come on. I've seen you look at me lately. I know when a guy isn't interested in just conversation."

"True again. You're wild, though, just wild. No one's ever—"

"No woman like me, you mean. Now shut up a minute and let me tell you about this little set-up Frank and I worked out. I'm going to let you make love to me, now, here, and we're going to really enjoy it."

He couldn't believe what he was hearing, but he adored it, her too maybe. He let her go on.

"Okay. I've given this a lot of thought, and you're going to get something special today, but I have a condition too. What do I love to do most?"

"Talk."

"Oh, the man has insight! Right, talk. So here's what's going to happen. You get to make love to me, but while you're taking off my things—slowly mind you!—Beth is going to get to babble about anything I want, and you will listen, but I assume that my body will be worth the price of my chatter, right?"

"Am I going to hear your analysis of James Joyce again?"

"In lengthy detail. Ready?"

He got to his feet, laughing, still half believing everything he was going through was a practical joke, and that Frank would pop out of the closet any second.

"Okay, you can start now. 'Portrait of an Artist' is vastly underrated. Critics say 'Ulysses' is Joyce's masterpiece work..."

"I'm listening," he said, as he began undoing the buttons of her blouse.

"...but 'Ulysses' never has characters that capture the imagination. They're, uh—that tickles—human abstracts, not real people we can live through. Molly Bloom. You can't really call her Molly like you can call other fictional characters by their—that's nice; uh, where was I?—by their, uhm, first names..."

"Shut up a second," he said. "I need to kiss you."

"We had an agreement," she said, as she put her lovely, winter-white bare arms around his neck, "but okay. I haven't finished about 'Ulysses' though."

The next day, when he got back home after his Statistics class, Frank gave him a letter. "Military address," he said. "Your friend maybe?"

The letter was indeed from Howard.

Dear James,

Hi. I'm at communications school here in West Virginia. We finished Basic a month ago, had a ten-day leave, and then wound up here. Fancy me a radioman! But the army said I was good in math. Is there a connection? Army logic.

We'll be at this place for a couple more weeks. So far we've learned code systems and simple electronic maintenance.

Basic was what I thought it would be, no sleep, marching all the time, physical training (I'm down to 180). If you have any college you have a tremendous advantage. In the service you don't question anything.

The guys who have the roughest times are some of the big-city blacks and a lot of poor whites from Appalachia. They can barely write their names, and the sergeants really grind on them. One guy in our outfit just couldn't take it, so he went AWOL. He got fifty miles away, by hitchhiking, then decided to take a bus. Only thing was, he couldn't read the name on it, and it brought him right back to base.

You wouldn't believe how ignorant of the war most men are. 95% I'd say have never even questioned it, or questioned anything for that matter, and the army never gives anybody time to think about anything. One day on the firing range it dawned on me that my rifle might be used for killing someone some day, a living Vietnamese. I'd gotten so into the procedures of lining up a target, it hadn't dawned on me.

What bugs the army the most these days, I gather, are the civilian coffee houses draft resistance groups have set up in G.I. towns like this one. (I'm writing you while sitting in one). The army can't do anything about them, and the people serve you free coffee and doughnuts. There's always plenty of anti-war literature around, but nobody forces it on you—unlike the army—so a lot of guys pick it up and read it. Needless to say, nobody takes it back to base!

I don't know where we're heading from here. The prospects don't look good even though I've applied for duty in Germany.

Drop me a line if you get a chance. My APO address is on the envelope.

Howard

He was finishing the letter when Frank came into the apartment. "There's a huge anti-war March on Washington being organized," Frank told him. He tossed him the paper he'd bought. "Looks like people don't want to wait for Nixon to act."

They were interrupted by a dunning racket of rock music from the floor above them. It was shaking the old plaster walls of the apartment house.

"God, what is that?"

"Marcus again, I guess," Frank answered. "Stoned silly. It's your turn to play the building's cop."

"At three in the afternoon, on Wednesday? What's happened to him?"

"Gave up! Tossed in the books, decided to have fun for the rest of the semester. Trying a lot of chemicals, peyote last week."

He went upstairs, knocked, and opened the door, knowing Marcus might be stretched out on a couch, immobilized, as he frequently was, and was now. "Gotta turn your stereo down, Marcus," he announced, as he walked across the room and adjusted the volume.

"No problem, James. Want some?" From the sofa he held up a joint, waving it in limp time to a contorted musical phrase by Jimi Hendrix.

"Keep this up, you'll get drafted you know." He stopped as he was about to exit.

"Canada," he heard. "All planned. Take care." The pillowed face was puffy-looking, and the eyes were having trouble focusing.

Sad, he thought, as he shut the door behind him. What a waste! And so many Marcuses were doing likewise on campus.

To friends he and Beth had become something of a couple, spending more idle hours together. But Beth was reluctant to get too involved. She had a career to think of, she told him. They were both too young to be too serious.

He cherished their hours together and didn't push her, not sure enough of his own commitment either to risk something. But they both knew that if either of them developed an interest in someone else, jealousy might suddenly be there in one of them, against their better wishes.

She had a theory—it wasn't hers actually, she admitted, but an idea of her mother—that guys didn't really mature till they got past their twenties. They needed to get rid of all their restlessness before settling down.

"Sounds like that stupid old 'Never Trust Anyone Over Thirty' stuff," he came back at her. They were in a Greek restaurant, in a warm, rear corner, protected against a cold end-of-March day, and he felt like teasing her. "And what if I wait around only to find you're some hag?"

"Then I'd take you in, pot-belly and all," she teased back. "Hey, listen to this idea, seriously, that my Psych prof said last week. He thinks our generation's growing older faster than previous ones. We've aged prematurely because of all we've been through, the assassinations and Vietnam. What do you think?"

"I think you'd be the prettiest thirty-year old hag on the block," he said, refusing to change the subject.

The student newspaper, *The Clarion*, had a story announcing the university was terminating its government grants for military purposes. Campus protest leaders were calling the decision a major victory.

Frank and he, who had been taking a class together near the Horton Research Center, noticed the change immediately. The student pickets who'd been ringing its entrance from January to March were gone.

"Can it actually be?" Frank said. "Somebody's finally listening?"

"They had to," he said. "Old Chinese proverb: So much writing on wall, wall fall over."

Frank, whose political instincts were always better than his, reminded him that walls could easily be white-washed before they crumbled.

On TV reporters were carrying daily reports about the developments for a protest march on Washington. It looked like thirty thousand people were going to be present in May for three days of demonstrating.

On the same program were photos of European heads of state who, that week, called for the U.S. to cease using napalm.

Every night there were images of the war itself: a photo snapped just as a captured suspect felt the impact of a captor's bullet entering his head; a girl, about ten years old, racing toward the camera, naked, her clothing burned off by napalm, which was still flaming in the background; body bags in battle areas, next to troops whose eyes showed a haggard emptiness.

The war was suddenly on campus too.

"Get your stuff! Hurry! The anti-Dow demonstrations have blown sky-high!" Frank came into the library, where James was studying, packing up his things for him as he talked. Then they were outside, his athletic roommate setting a pace he could barely keep up with, as they headed up a long campus hill and the place where Dow Chemical was recruiting future employees in a campus building.

Nearing the demonstration site, they heard sirens. Students were racing with them and past them in the opposite direction, and they smelled something, as something stung their eyes.

"Tear gas! They beat us up!" A woman student raced past, her cheeks smudged. "Don't go near there!" she warned. She was coughing heavily.

Frank and he came over the crest of the hill and stopped abruptly. Half a football field from them, below them in a natural basin, were helmeted and masked police, who were pushing some students into a paddy wagon. Other police vehicles skirted the wagon as reinforcement.

At the entrance to the Social Science building a phalanx of more masked police formed a human barrier line across its front entrance.

The building's normal occupants were being escorted from another entryway.

Upwind, in an area that was a small garden, a group of twenty or thirty protestors were milling about, watching the police. They had handkerchiefs over their mouths, having been targeted earlier by the tear gas.

In surrounding buildings, people were crowded against the windows, watching.

Television crews were on the same hill as Frank and him, and were filming. Three police officers without masks were trying to restrain the crews from going toward the center of action.

A group of a hundred students like themselves, onlookers, stood watching everything else. But as they were watching, a rock sailed over their heads toward the police cars. Frank and he, like others in their crowd, sensed instantly that they might be seen as people who threw the rock, so they made a lateral dash to more neutral ground, in a nearby parking lot. When they got their breath, they saw three police chasing an individual from the area they'd just been in. Then the police withdrew, the individual waving at them, taunting them, laughing. He had on what looked like an old high school sports jacket, with a skull and crossbones on its back. On his long hair was a navy watch cap.

"Frank, I think I know that guy!"

"You're kidding."

"No, he's from my hometown. Randy! We were friends all through school."

"I wouldn't go renew acquaintances right now." His roommate was looking at the rock-thrower with the same fascination he was having. Neither of them had ever seen someone so defiant of authority.

Within a week the campus had quieted down, but only superficially. The protesters had vanished from the Social Science building, but small groups of demonstrators would appear sporadically. Missing now was the pluckiness and festive spontaneity of earlier events. Everyone had become serious.

All week long *The Clarion* carried a series of editorials. Over coffee he was quoting parts of the latest one, to Beth.

"Listen," he said:

> "'*For a week now campus police have tried to assert that the Dow Protest demonstration was the work of outside agitators, perhaps communists. The sole evidence for this view, it turns out, was the presence of a car with California license plates, parked forty yards from the scene.*'"

Beth was open-mouthed across from him, as he went on:

> "'*Claims like this raise serious questions: Are the police so self-deceived as to believe their assumptions? Are the claims a deliberate strategy meant to draw attention away from the issue of the use of napalm and agent orange? The Dow Demonstration…*'"

"I hear ten buses are going to D.C., to the March," Beth said. "Before things blew here, last week, there were only two."

"Frank's going. He decided yesterday."

"Why don't you go along?"

"Oh, that'd go over great with my folks!"

"Your dad will find out sooner or later, James. You know he will."

"I know. I'm dreading it."

"So go. You want to."

"I do and don't. Nixon's been in office only three months. He's withdrawn some troops. Maybe we need to give this some time to play out a little."

"I hear Harris Point in your voice, words you don't believe." Beth's expression, veering to a tease for a second, went to sympathy instead.

"I just can't stand it," he said to Beth and Frank, as he dished up pasta for the three of them. "I sit there next to that jerk at the literature table, and I just want to turn to him and ask him outright what he thinks he's doing. 'Do you like being a spy, Creighton? And by the way, what's your real name?'"

"But remember we might use him later," Frank reminded him, "for our benefit."

Beth grated some more Parmesan onto her linguini. "I know what you mean though. It seems so phony, playing the game. Plus there's always the thought that we could turn him around, to get dear old Wallace to see how screwed up he is, ratting on people."

"Hopeless," Frank put in. "He's paid well to believe the government's nonsense, that fucker!"

"He sat down next to me, right next to me this morning and conversed like it was the most normal thing in the world. At first I felt like I wanted to race across the room to put as much space between us as possible...."

"Run away from the leper," Beth suggested. "That's natural."

"The old feeling of spooks all around us, like when we were young and Oswald took out JFK!" Frank mimicked rooting out enemies, by lifting a corner of the tablecloth.

"Then I had a different impulse," James said, "to strangle the guy right then and there. Really!

I'm serious."

"Not that you'd ever act on the feeling, right?" Beth said. "That's what the government would love all of us to do."

"Why don't you do this?" Frank offered. "Chat up our spy friend about his past and his fake major in art, to make him feel uncomfortable. Not too much, mind you, or he'll get wise to our being wise to him. Just keep him off balance. At least it will keep you from going crazy."

"Not a bad idea," he said. "I'll try that." Beth's hand was on his briefly, steadying him.

At Wendy's urging he decided to go to church on Easter Sunday, and his going pulled his dad along. Before service, in front of the church, his mother reveled in the idea of them all as the heart of the church flock.

During the final prayer, when Pastor Allen asked the congregation to pray for those at home, and in distant lands, too, he could feel his father's spine stiffen, next to him.

They almost got through the ham dinner without any strife, but then his dad asked if he'd seen Randy on campus. He heard he had transferred there.

James said he'd seen him once. Then he made the mistake of describing where, at the anti-Dow demonstration with Randy throwing rocks at the police.

His sister desperately tried to steer the conversation to neutral ground. Randy was wild like that his last year in high school, she said.

But his father had found an opening. What was this anti-napalm thing? he wanted to know. He'd seen it on the news the night it happened, the demonstration.

His mother's lips pinched, anticipating the worst. But there was no way to pass off an answer lightly.

"Most of the students think the use of napalm is inhumane. It's a jelly that Dow Chemical Company makes, and it fries the skin in seconds."

"Bunch of softy draft dodgers–!" his dad started in, but he cut him off.

"There's no way to control it. Whole villages of innocent peasants blister into nothing from it."

"War's war!" his dad retorted.

"So we should pour cyanide into the enemy's drinking water? Use mustard gas again?" He hated and loved what he'd said, antagonism and intellectual argument—couldn't stop the sentence.

"Why not?"

By now his mother had started to tear up, and he felt he should back off, but something inside him kept him going. Years of feelings roared to be out of him. "Dow's making tons of money off Agent Orange too!"

"Anything wrong with some company making money?"

"It's hurting our own troops. The whole landscape dies for decades."

"Christ, you–!"

His mother was flying out of the room, and Wendy was going after her. Their exits made no difference to either his father or him.

"Christ, you got taken in by that liberal crap! My own son, a brain with no brains! They ought to draft you, and then you'd see what's good about napalm!"

He waited till his Dad paused in his tirade. He got up, his chest futilely trying to chain the emotions he'd felt for two years, as he gathered his plate and silver to take to the kitchen. Then he stopped and looked at his father. "The war's a tragic mistake," he said. "I won't go."

An hour later he was still driving around town, letting the anger and pain of the afternoon try to work itself out. He'd known for a long time that he and his father would have the confrontation. But he'd sensed, too, that when it happened it would be more jolting than expected. And it had been. He'd seen a willful ignorance in his father that he'd found infuriating. Then he felt pain at his role of a son not conforming to his dad's beliefs.

The worst pain came from placing his mother in the position of having to shuttle between quarreling husband and offspring, now. She didn't deserve what she would be getting, but neither could she avoid it.

"I won't go!" was a different reality now, also, especially here in his home town. Maybe his dad would try to keep the statement quiet, out of shame, but probably word would circulate soon about his defiance. In Harris Point, where serving in wars had been an honorable business, he would be talked about as a selfish traitor. People he'd known all his life would stop saying hello to him or wave lamely at him and slink away into stores or cars. Sooner or later he was on his way to becoming an outcast.

If he became a conscientious objector, he would face a long and wearing ordeal of legality. His Quaker lawyer friend, who advised the students on campus, had described it to him once: the filing of paper after paper, the processing of information, the debilitating series of draft board and court hearings. People who opposed him would look upon him as an annoyance. He wouldn't be allowed to say that he wouldn't serve because the war was wrong; that wasn't an acceptable legal defense. He would have to say that his god told him not to serve, the Quaker noted wryly, at the very moment he was questioning why any god would have allowed the monstrous thing in Asia to happen.

The government had endless resources. It was larger than he thought, massive really. It would make life miserable enough that he would have an impulse to give in. If he did, he would hate himself in the long run.

He nursed an incongruous thought, a fleeting but fervid wish for the military to win the war in the next months, with whatever it took. But the "whatever it took" meant the further destruction of a whole countryside, people, and culture. No choice there!

His thoughts took another sick turn: if the destruction was already happening on a large scale, then what difference did total destruction make? It was logical. Perversely neat, the way Washington thought these days. *Destroy a village to save it.*

He drove another half hour, telling himself to calm down, *calm down.* He knew that he would get past these moments. But here in his home town, ten minutes from the house he'd grown up in, he felt as far away as he possibly could be.

He got back to campus before the March on Washington. That weekend, looking for Frank in the TV coverage, he heard the reporters say that more than double the amount of people expected were showing up.

The camera scanned the massive crowd, the voice of the reporter commenting that the protesters represented all walks of life, a broad spectrum of American society by occupation, race, and age.

It was clear, the reporter said, that the protest showed dissatisfaction with the war was spreading to every segment of the population. The dissenters were organized and could mobilize on a national scale, and they were carefully schooled in the techniques of non-violence Martin Luther King used.

Another reporter came on to say that for every four demonstrators there was a policeman, federal marshal, or national guardsman.

Later there were shots of the demonstrators marching through the streets, being guided by their parade organizers, crossing Arlington Memorial Bridge and moving on to the Pentagon, where the sheer bulk of the crowds pushed against temporary restraining fences. Above them were hundreds of placards saying things like U. OF CHICAGO SAYS NO! VANDERBILT: WITHDRAW NOW! BRING DOWN THE WAR MACHINE! QUAKERS DEMAND PEACE! MOTHERS AGAINST THE WAR! MACHINISTS LOCAL 12, SAN DIEGO! NOPE, NOPE! and SENIORS SAY NO!

At his sister's graduation, his father took a huge number of pictures with a new camera he'd bought. By keeping busy, Wendy said, he didn't have to talk at all with his wife or kids, and that had been his behavior since Easter. He was spending almost every evening in his work-room downstairs, but neither she nor their mother could see any effect of his being there.

He hugged his sister in her graduation gown and told her she'd do well in college.

When he told his mother the next day that he'd gotten a summer job at a boys' camp, as an assistant director, his mother couldn't hide her relief. "It would be nice to have you here," she tried to say.

"But it'd be terrible to have Dad and me fighting all summer, wouldn't it?"

She shook her head yes, her dismay eating at her.

Wendy sent him photos at the camp. In the pictures of her, she was a proud graduate.

In one shot his mother and father were together, but both seemed to show manufactured pleasantry. In another his father had slipped into the lockjaw determination he displayed most of the previous year. Wendy, in another, looked like she was propping up her mother. In the one photo of him, alone, that Wendy insisted be taken, he saw that he'd gone to the graduation ceremony with his hair uncombed.

In the trying-to-be-festive face of the photo was a weight that elongated its natural shape. His gray blue eyes looked almost black—a flaw in the film, he wondered, or too much lived through, too early in life?

Don't be bitter, he told himself. *Other generations have gone through worse. But what more does this generation have to go through?*

Vacation Country, 1969, Summer

He watched the campers take their canoes from the lake and tie them to the launch ramp. It was mid-July, and he decided to linger five minutes before following the young people—ten and eleven-year-old's accompanied by their teen-age counselors—to the camp's cabins and mess hall.

Tomorrow this group would be gone, and he'd have a three-day weekend. Beth was coming with her family, on vacation, Beth, whom he missed more than he could have imagined.

Out on the lake he could see in the far distance the pair of loons that were part of the late after-noon landscape. Placidly, they moved west where the water narrowed before emptying out into an adjoining river. At this time of day the water calmed and was free of human traffic.

How different this summer had been from the previous one! He'd been at home then, sickened almost weekly by things on television.

In June, home from the university, he watched the grim recap of Robert Kennedy's shooting and slow death in the hospital–this on the heels of Martin Luther King being snipered away, on the motel balcony in Memphis, in April.

How much more? he asked himself. There really was a conspiracy to eliminate those associated with the anti-war movement, wasn't there? *No, no, of course not, don't be silly James.* But then why did the idea ring so bone-marrow true? On campus radicals had been saying for years that the FBI was corrupt because Hoover saw every Negro as a commie infiltrator. Really, the Director was deranged about black people!

But then in a dozen cities blacks took to madness themselves, not communist blacks but average Joe Citizens setting fires to buildings, smashing storefronts, looting businesses. A whole section of Los Angeles flamed for almost a week, raw, dirty billows of smoke spiraling into the blue sky above. At week's end residents whose relatives had torched supermarkets were angrily asking who was going to supply them food.

The war abroad continued, on TV story after story, body counts included, a thing hanging on and on in its fifth year. No change, just more of the same stalemate, a huge superpower trying to swat democracy into a jungle patch. There was talk now of Vietnamizing the war, as if it had been somewhere else. Folly layered upon stupidity, stupidity slathered on ignorance!

In August came the Democratic convention in Chicago. God, that convention! Metaphors for it died instantly, as blood puddled the ground at Grant Park and on Chicago streets.

They had no idea what was coming, the thousands of protestors, surrounded by thuggy Chicago cops and National Guard troops, who waded into the crowds, their white night sticks flying. James shuddered at the TV coverage of people who tried to flee but couldn't, with the area boxed in. Two tanks threatened to crush anyone in their tracks, as the camera flashed on panic-pale faces. Then the camera itself seemed out of control, its operator himself fleeing.

The TV anchor cut in to say that while the police were attacking the demonstrators in the streets, other police were ransacking Gene McCarthy's campaign headquarters, for no reason. The Chicago police wouldn't admit to any of their ransacking taking place, even when shown footage of it. The mayor, Richard Daley, blithely proclaimed that nothing was wrong on the city's streets. *No, nothing at all, Mister Mayor, for god's sake. That red stuff on the ground—type A, O, or whatever—it came out of the sky in a rainstorm. Maybe you'd like to see it in a microscope.*

He recalled the random thoughts he'd had then, twelve months before. What he was seeing bore no resemblance to anything he'd been taught about governments and their citizens. In this one citizens (clergy and housewives included) were mauled and bludgeoned by those in authority. The principle of law was tear gas and a riot stick; the right of appeal, the opportunity to look up from the pavement and see a gestapo-like boot coming down on your already smashed cheek.

He stayed in his room or went over to Howard's those days to watch most of the news. At home, he knew, he and his father would clash over what they were seeing. Only once, on the third convention day when his dad called the protestors a bunch of lazy bums, did he react to his elder's words, letting his voice gather intensity and his anger come out. "They're demonstrators!" he almost shouted, passing through the living room. "They believe in something! They've got a right to do that!"

How far back in time! On the lake one of the loons had dived, in that long underwater passage that loons did, and now it reappeared, having gone under the better part of five minutes. It had come up for air.

They'd all been under a long time too, he thought. This summer's oxygen felt wonderful.

When she drove up, he hadn't known how to act. He'd kissed her but in a way that might have seemed half-hearted.

She asked to be shown the camp, so he gave her a tour, but the chit-chat during their walk seemed to delay what he wanted to express. What held him back, also, was the fear that he'd press her too hard, sending her into recoil withdrawal. He remembered her statements the previous spring, that both of them were too young to think about anything permanent.

And yet being away from her for six weeks, and being with her now again, convinced him he was in love with her, beyond reason. Beneath his mundane, factual explanations of camp life was his nearly delirious feeling about being with her again, holding her hand, touching her. *So sweet*!

She was driving them back to the cabin her family had rented. He and she, her younger sister, and her parents—they were all going to have dinner together.

Now, on the way there, they were talking a little, but she was surprisingly quiet too. There were lapses of silence, mysterious if not sinister.

"You seem different," she said finally. "Like you're not entirely sure you want to see me."

"I'm sorry it shows, but it's not what you think."

"Cryptic, James. You want me to drive you back to camp, let you out and call it quits? Is there someone else?"

"There's no one else. That's the problem."

He could see her trying to grasp the paradox, not able to work through it. He studied her face as she navigated the pine forest's roads.

"The problem is that I can't stop myself," he went on. "I love you. I love you so much I can't stand it. I wanted to respect your need for not rushing into something deeper. But you're in my thoughts all the time. I read your letters twenty times a day, I carry one around in my pocket all day long, and I'm always seeing us together. I can't think of me without thinking of you with me."

He took a deep, sigh-filled breath, watching the roadway, afraid to look at her. *I've scared her off.*

The roadway slowed in front of the car, as she stopped. "Can you come round to my side of the car?" She was looking at him in a way she never had.

She got out, he came round the front fender, baffled, and she put her arms around him, speaking into his ear, barely facing him. "It's happened, hasn't it? We thought we could be cool about us, and here we are about to throw ourselves at each other forever. God, what a couple of idiots we are, for letting it happen."

"For thinking it wouldn't," he said. He lifted her face, and then they held each other so tightly they had trouble finding breath.

All through dinner, they gave each other quick and happy glances, as though not sure everything had happened.

Her mother talked as much as Beth, so there was constant friendly competition for air time, and Beth's sister, a sixteen-year-old, was a lively conversationalist in her own right. The exception seemed to be Beth's father, who carried a quiet thoughtfulness with him. But when an idea piqued him, he could become as animated as the rest of them. The whole family thrived on discussion.

At meal's end Jane Stephens announced that she, Jess, and Amy were off to a nearby town, to see a movie. He didn't know what to make of this, nor of the moment when Beth and her mother stood near the car and hugged, like overly-friendly spies.

"What was that all about?" They were alone together, his arms circling her from behind. "Shouldn't we have gone with everybody? It's a terrible film, I hear."

"My mom wanted us to have this time," she said. "Ten minutes after we walked in, she knew we were in love."

"How on earth—?"

"Mom and I have this special thing. She thinks you're wonderful."

"But she's only known me an hour."

"Doesn't matter. Leave those." She took the dishes he'd picked up from the table. She turned around and kissed him, not in the methodically sensuous way she usually did, but hard, recklessly. "Damn, this feels good."

I just don't know where the limits should be," he was saying. It was the Stephenses last night of vacation, and they were gathered again at the small cabin table. Jess Stephens had taken great pride in the grilled chicken he'd done.

"The priests," James went on, "who chain themselves to military installation gates, I don't have any problem with them at all. It's right in line with Gandhi and King. You break the law and accept the consequences openly. Dramatize the moral issue!"

"Make a deliberate public example, sure," Beth's mother put in. "No different than picketing a bank sucking tons of money out of South Africa." She was speaking from experience, he knew. Early in their acquaintance, months before, Beth filled him in on her parents' activist pasts.

"But this business of bombing draft board offices, that's where I'd have a problem."

"Doesn't everything depend on the context of the time, James?" Jess questioned. "If Congress takes no responsibility, then people go to more extreme measures–have to, maybe."

"But lawbreaking invites disorder. Did last summer's riots in the cities do anything positive?"

"Woke people up, maybe." Beth's dad sounded only half confident in his theory.

"Turned people off," Beth took up the challenge. "Blacks became looters, not victims."

Jane took a turn: "Suppose the war goes on for another five years...."

"It won't, it can't." Beth's sister felt the need to contribute. "Right, Mom?"

"Think so, hon'?" Turning to the others but not completely away from her youngest, she posed a hypothetical: "There's the morality issue, don't you all think? Like when we fire-bombed German cities at the end of World War Two. So, say we—"

"Good example, grotesque stuff," Jess said, reinvigorated. "Say we firebomb Hanoi, the city itself. No military purpose for what we do, but just say we do it, off civilians en masse."

"Bomb the hell out of 'em. Kill a hundred thousand in a day." Beth picked up her father's thread. "An administration clearly immoral. Just feeding Nixon's ego!"

"Sure makes bombing a draft board office seem reasonable to me," Jane concluded. "Not that I'd do it myself."

At morning mail-call he got a long letter from Howard.

July 20, 1969

Dear James,

I really appreciate your letters. Sometimes they take a month to get here, but that doesn't matter.

So far I've mainly been in Saigon, a big city, very modern looking. It's filled with bicycles, motorcycles, people and more people. Some of the buildings look like American skyscrapers, and some of the night spots look like our discotheques.

Out in the country, conditions are very different. People live in primitive huts and work rice fields. There's nothing like our plumbing, and kids generally don't go to a school except for a couple of years. People have little contact with anyone outside their hamlet, and they have no idea why American planes defoliate or bomb their fields. Saigon's air force drops leaflets to explain, but since most people can't read, the message never gets through. The VC come through, demanding rice, and sometimes kidnaping village leaders.

Then our troops come through and confiscate the rest of the rice and interrogate everybody. Or if we don't confiscate the rice, we poison it with that agent orange stuff, so the people on lands they've occupied for hundred of years have to move.

Either way, the peasants get caught between, not knowing which side to believe. They'd just like to flip back the clock a couple of hundred years, not that there are clocks here, if you know what I'm saying.

The army treats all the Vietnamese with suspicion. That may be good from a military standpoint, but I'm not sure. A new friend of mine, who worked at U.S. headquarters in Saigon, says that Americans there don't even try to learn Vietnamese. All the American officials have their personal interpreters.

So far our duty has been mostly non-combat, and it should stay that way. I hope. Five of the guys in my company were transferred last month, and two were killed in a search-and-destroy mission.

Do I sound scared? I shouldn't be. Even if my unit gets transferred, I'll probably end up at battalion headquarters manning the radio.

Bye for now. Say hi to all the folks in Harris Point when you get back home before heading off to school again. Boy, do I ever miss Jennifer.

Howard

"Man, the Lake Valley thing was something! Seven bands, two days. So much grass, Security just gave up trying to control it. Other stuff too, speed mainly."

"Lots of people?" He saw now that the hitchhiker he'd picked up outside of town, on his way back to camp, was older than he'd thought, maybe twenty, not seventeen. The guy's zeal for drugs was frightening.

"Zillions! Everybody groovin' on each other, though. You know?" His passenger was reaching into a battered army rucksack that seemed almost part of a uniform hitchhikers were wearing these days. There were tons of them this summer, roaming the country. One he picked up a week ago said he'd been on the road for seven weeks.

"Want an apple?"

"No thanks. I just ate, half hour ago. You a student?"

"I dunno."

When he looked baffled, the hitchhiker realized what he'd said and snickered. "It sounds confusing," he admitted. "My folks want me to continue, so I'll probably go back to campus. But I gotta see the world. Find myself."

Slowing down for a turn, he remembered Beth scoffing at revelations like that he'd just heard. More and more they were running into young people in search of themselves by bolting off to distant utopias, sometimes in the middle of a desert. Beth, with her honed sense of irony, called them the barefoot wanderers.

Now the hitchhiker was launching into a theme they also heard a lot lately, about how the world was corrupt, fixated on materialist things. Beth and he, achievers both, had done a lot of rolling of the eyes, hearing similar spiels.

"Sure you won't have an apple?"

"Thanks, no."

"Tastes even better if you don't have to pay for it."

"Pardon?" He wasn't sure he was hearing right.

"I ripped it off, from that general store in town. Next to the bait shop."

His passenger looked to him half-winking, egging him on, as though he should share a story of his own petty thievery somewhere. What an outrageous assumption, he thought, that all young people had a right to shoplift. No, not a right, an obligation!

Back on campus four months before, he and Frank had listened to a socialist proclaiming similar claptrap, and Frank had worked his response into an ongoing comic routine. One day he'd do mock-apologies to Beth and him, saying that he'd tell his capitalist-exploiter boss to screw off any day now, but the time just wasn't right, the stars were badly aligned. Next day, he'd do a revery to the effect that he'd changed his mind, that even capitalists could be converted, so he was going to buy his boss a copy of *Das Kapital.* Day three, he'd act out a phoney identity crisis: Buying the book for his pig boss was a great idea, but publishers were automating workers out of jobs, so he probably should boycott buying books, including Marx's masterpiece. Oh, he was torn up inside! In agony! Maybe he'd choose a life of poverty, like Tolstoy, if he could have a hamburger now and then.

Wonderfully subtle Frank! But his hitchhiker had no subtlety at all and was just a rubber stamp for whoever could tell him it was okay to be dishonest. After a moment he said: "That store you stole from. That would be the Olsons' place. Woman about fifty? Bleached blonde?" He realized he was drifting into small-talk and didn't want to be. "You do that often? Shoplift?"

"Hell yes. Payin' back all those rich guys for rippin' us off all the time! Fucking us over!"

The words went on, and he listened to them for a moment, his anger roiling. Then he slowed down, coming to a stop on the roadside.

"You'll have to get out here," he said."I'm turning left."

"Hey, that's cool too," the hitchhiker said. "I go with the flow."

"No," he said quietly, and it was the other person's turn to be confused now, as he got out.

"Uh...thanks," he said. "Take care. Ciao."

Before he drove off, he looked at the eyes beneath the traveler's bandannaed hair, trying to fathom some shred of integrity that probably wasn't there. "That Peg Olson–she reads to the elderly two nights a week," he said, "at the old folks' home."

The remark, intended to fire some guilt into a faulty conscience, took a trajectory away, into meaningless space.

"Who?" he heard behind him, as he drove off. It was clear he and his hitchhiker had been talking different languages, generated maybe by different types of brains. In the rear-view mirror, he could see his former passenger settling down near a tree, next to the road's shoulder. No hassle, real cool, no problem. No hope, James thought.

"I'm beginning to think you're more right than I once thought," he was saying, "about how life is changing."

He was back home for a few weeks, between his summer job and heading off to Chicago to see Beth before classes started again on campus. Helping his mother in the kitchen, he related his experience with the hitchhiker, and they went from there to the subject of Woodstock. Not having TV access at the camp, he'd seen a rerun of the event for the first time, only the day before, and was stunned by the images: a hundred thousand people taking up hobo residence in a vast farmland; rock music deafening and often shriekingly off-key; rains cascading for hours onto festival-goers who reveled in the ensuing mud; people standing naked in the human hordes as if the nudity was the most natural thing in the world.

"Do your friends behave like that at school?" his mother wanted to know. "I worry for Wendy more than for you. She's younger, more likely to fall into bad company. And now there's that L-D-S drug—" Her fingers came down hard as she cut a carrot.

"L-S-D, Mom."

"Whatever it is. Kids take it and think they can fly?"

"Uh-huh. A lot of them feel alienated from everything—minorities who feel cheated and people who hate the war."

"There you go again on that war. I tell myself it's not that bad."

"It is. But there's a group of people, too, who just seem to want thrills all the time, kids with a lot of money. They've never had to work for anything. For them the war's an excuse."

"Oh, dear. You mean our generation was too good to you."

"Not you, you and dad, you know that. Wendy and I always appreciated what you've given us."

"You know, I wonder how many other mothers like me worry all the time. I don't think I ever stop, and I'm afraid of what I'm doing to myself. Oh, it's silly, like I'm going to frighten myself into having cancer or something."

The thought of his mother being gone caught him off guard. He wanted to tell her that things would change for the better, but he didn't know that he believed they would, so he held back. Washing lettuce, he fell silent, sobered by his hard contemplation.

On Campus, Fall 1969

Right before school Beth brought him to her house in Ryan's Park. She was going to do a practice-teaching internship that would keep her off-campus the whole semester, in a public high school two hundred miles away. So they cherished their lazy free time together, days in Chicago at the Art Institute and the Aquarium, nights in the clubs on Rush Street. Then it was back to the university for him.

He was so used to her being with him on campus, he kept looking for her in their old haunts. But instead of finding her, one day he found Randy, at the Chow Haus, at its bar, with hamburgers sizzling in the background on the grill.

They shook hands. Randy's hair, he saw, was receding–he was going to be bald early. But he still had the prominent square chin Harris Point girls once liked. On the counter in front of him was a stack of currency, put there to impress anyone who passed, and he had a nice tan, which, he explained, came from lots of elapsed time at the Harris Point Country Club.

"That private college didn't suit you?"

"Place was a vacuum of social life," Randy grinned. "Cute blondes but all of them shy and sincere about everything. And the profs were too demanding. Double whammy, boy!"

Listening to his former friend, he was brought back to high school recollections. Randy always had an enviable glibness, a fraternity row gloss from the 50's, but he also had a superiority streak. If he joined anything, all others had to sign on as his drones.

Easily bored too, he was—with things, activities, people—and James remembered talking one time with Howard, discussing whether the boredom came from Randy's being too intelligent for his own good or from a selfish need to be entertained. They decided on the latter.

He'd been majoring in P.E, he was saying. Maybe was going to change to Art Education. Or Biology. Naming the possibilities, he saw the folly of his speculation and turned it into a joke: "Or Political Science. Comp Lit, Nuclear Physics. So what's new with Harris Point's Einstein, James? Still burning through the pages of books?"

He told him yes but he was involved with a woman, too, someone he'd probably marry eventually. He was tempted to reveal his anti-war work, but that involved mention of seeing Randy throwing rocks at the police the previous spring, near the Social Science Building. He didn't want to do that. Caution was telling him to keep arm's length distance from his fellow high school grad.

Love,

Am I exhausted! Never dreamed teaching could take so much out of a person. All the faculty tell me it's just something you go through the first year, since you have so much to prepare and so little time from one day to the next, plus papers to grade in between, so I crash into bed every night at midnight.

Love, you know how I love to talk. Well, I thought I could just open my mouth, and the class hours would pass, but my first day I planned a forty minute lecture, and it lasted twenty! The rest of the time I hemmed and hawed, repeating myself, which my supervisor says I have to do with sophomores anyway, but—Where was I? Ah!—so I've learned to draw students out by keeping my own yakking to a minimum, which is hard, very hard for me, but it's working a lot better, and I'm getting confidence these days, finally.

One of the great things about the sophomores is that they still have some innocence although not too much these days, so some of them confide in me. A big football player has a crush on me, so says the American History teacher down the hall from my classroom. Jealous?

Gotta go. Have to teach this wimpy story tomorrow about a shrinking violet woman. Required reading. Yech! I'll try not to show my lack of enthusiasm.

I want a warm body in my cold bed. Can you suggest someone?

Beth

He was low on money that week, but he borrowed enough from Frank to send her half a dozen roses.

It was back, and they were too, the military research and the pickets around Horton Hall, Frank told him, returning from Advanced Biology Concepts one afternoon in late September. Normally his roommate was a person who kept emotions in check, but on this rainy day he stomped into the apartment hard, thumping the boards beneath the worn carpet. The strength of his soccer player legs made the sounds seem like pounding during construction work.

"The governor appointed two new regents," he said. "They're hardcore business people who want the university to take in all the money it can get!"

"Here we go again."

"Worst thing was that they tried to slip it by everybody. But a math major with a journalism minor rooted it out. Shit, James!"

He went the long way to a class the next day to see the picketing, and for the first time he took a good look at the structure which had been such a bitter symbol to so many students and university staff. Horton Hall was a late-forties structure, with a few token flares on the cornices. Except for a renovated facade on the main entrance, its six floors looked bare-bones, as though it hadn't been funded adequately when built. Looking into its windows, he could see that the interior had never been updated or even painted.

"Shabby!" he commented to Frank that night. "You'd think with all the money the math department's getting, they'd pump some into the facility."

"No imagination," Frank said sourly. "If they can't connect fresh paint to dirty plaster, how the hell will they ever link their work to killing Vietnamese?"

Dear James,

This may be a depressing letter. The last two days here have been real bad.

We've been on the edge of some fighting, not close but close enough anyway.

A couple of nights ago at an enlisted man's club in Saigon a bunch of us were drinking. Five or six marines were in a booth in back of us, and we all drank a lot for a long time.

We all got to talking to one another, and one of the marines, who'd gotten kind of loud, told us about a mission he was on a month ago. His platoon was out in the field and came into contact with an army platoon that had taken six Vietnamese women prisoner. The women were only suspects, and the army guys didn't know what to do with them, so the marines took them off their hands.

You can guess what that means. According to this guy, who was bragging about what had happened (really enjoying telling it, the bastard), the whole platoon worked over the women for five or six hours and then just wasted 'em. I won't tell you how, but when I heard how, I went out the back door of the bar and puked.

This is really only half the story. Yesterday, I'd put the rape and murder thing out of my mind somewhat because I had to try to keep my sanity. But then—I was on my way back from a field area, in a chopper. My buddies and I didn't know what was happening, but then it set down to pick up three army guys, one an interpreter, and two VC prisoners.

All of them got on, and then the interpreter started questioning the VC. Neither would talk, so two of the army goons finally dragged a VC over to the open door and threatened to shove him out.

We all just sat there watching, assuming that it was a good threat, but no sooner did they get the guy over there, they rifle-butted him in the back of his head—right out! It all happened so fast we just sat there flabbergasted. I mean there was this living person there, and then just like that he was gone, battered out at 2,000 feet. The VC might have been the day's garbage for all those army guys cared.

You can see why I'm low. You tell yourself that you're just putting in your time till you get home. You'll just take orders and not question anything that's done, it's all necessary. But there's a limit. You have to live with yourself when you get home, and how are you going to forget things you hear and see?

Howard

P.S. Incidentally, some of the guys have stories that would make mine look like comic book stuff. There's one rumor floating around about a massacre where our troops wiped out 300 people in a village, for no reason at all.

Dear Beth,

My lovely dynamo, it's great that you took over the debate team when your colleague got hospitalized for the rest of the semester, but save some time and energy for us. No, never mind. I know you couldn't give less than 100%, so I'll live with your extra commitment. When you come here, I'll rub your back in all the right places to relieve your fatigue.

Will your family accept me more with my new picketer credentials? The trial for the fifteen protestors arrested during the anti-Dow demonstration is going on this week, and to show support we've set up a line outside the federal courthouse in town. I felt a little weird out there on the street for the first time, but then everything seemed natural. In fact there's something cathartic about taking a public stand. You go from feeling like an oddball eccentric to thinking of yourself as the public's conscience.

Why am I telling you that? When your folks brought you along on those civil rights marches five years ago, you must have felt what I'm talking about.

The local district attorney wants to limit the trial testimony to the issue of disorderly conduct, blocking a public entry. The defense is arguing that the disorderliness occurred when the police closed the other end of the corridor, creating an explosive situation.

The defense is also trying to get into the trial DOW Chemical's continued manufacture of war chemicals. The judge won't permit that, probably, but the papers here are reporting for the first time how extensively napalm and agent orange are being used. So the trial is having a good effect.

In all of your busy paper-grading time have you followed the plans for that national moratorium being organized? At the end of October? There'll be a big do at the field house here, since it holds fifteen thousand. I'm part of a group organizing other events—poetry readings at the Arts and Letters Building, lectures on napalm at Science Hall, symposiums on agent orange at the med school. Some of the participants will be Vietnam vets who have turned against the war.

Just think, last spring there were fifty thousand people in Washington for the March. This fall there'll be fifteen thousand here alone. We're being heard, Love. Our numbers are growing.

I do study, Love, and go to classes. I haven't stopped being a student, but I had to drop Art History II since I was so committed to the Moratorium work.

Ten days till you're here. An eternity!

James

The first segment of the evening news showed a rubbled area in New York City. A reporter in front of it, against a barricade guarded by police, was explaining that a three-storey apartment on the site had been leveled by a bomb. "Police here," he said, "are fairly certain the explosion went off accidentally while the bomb was being constructed. Police are also convinced the bomb-makers were young revolutionaries."

The program cut to a news conference with the Secretary of Defense. "I am announcing today," he said, "the withdrawal of more units of military personnel from Vietnam. This reduces our forces to three hundred and seventy-five thousand men."

Later in the program a commentator appeared. "Earlier in this program," he said, "we presented two reports, on a bombing and a troop withdrawal.

"The Secretary of Defense's announcement seems to confirm that the system of government seems to be working. The powers of government have listened.

"On the other hand there is the view, dramatically emphasized by the revolutionaries, that the system is a fraud, an illusion.

"It would seem that the vast majority of Americans favor the first view. But it also seems to this observer that should President Nixon change course, we will see a significant shift in public behavior toward the revolutionary viewpoint.

"The issue is clearer today. Which alternative the people choose is more than ever up to the president."

He turned the small TV on, softly so he could hear but not so loud that she'd awaken. She'd arrived in town the previous night, and they were delirious being with one another again. They had a late dinner he'd fixed and then made long, caring love till two in the morning.

Today he planned for them to take a long afternoon walk along the campus's lakefront, in the early October air. But Beth woke, went back to sleep, and then repeated the cycle again. "That's me," she said groggily from her pillow. It was five-forty-five.

"What are you talking about?"

Her hand emerged from beneath the covers and one of her fingers pointed to the TV screen. "That thing there...."

He looked at the program a moment, where a camera was focused on a zoo elephant in some kind of medical difficulty, huge in photo perspective and breathing at sporadic intervals. A reporter was saying the animal was still sick but recovering.

"C'mon, you're not overweight. You never were."

"No, not weight! Energy. It might as well be me, Beth the Inert."

"You're pretty when you sleep," he said.

"I dreamed I was grading term papers," she said, "thousands of them! Kiss me, and I might get up."

The phone rang, and he answered, listening. "Okay," he said, briefly. "Thanks. It's the first album, right? Got it."

"What was that all about?"

"Tell you later."

They went out for hamburgers and beer, and on the way out of the restaurant, he and Frank steered her down a street she was unfamiliar with. Then they were up a back stairs to the fifth floor of a building half a block south of their own apartment.

"Where on earth are we going?" Beth wanted to know.

"To deliver an Otis Redding record," Frank said, but neither he nor James had anything like one tucked under an arm.

James told her: Otis Redding was a code word dropped during the phone call he got while they were in bed earlier. Their friends were warning them they were under surveillance.

They knocked and were met by a young student couple, who took them inside their apartment. Then the couple turned out the lights. "We usually wait five minutes," the woman, Serena, said. "That gives them time to think we've gone out."

They waited, and then James invited Beth over to a window, covered with a blind. "Stand here, to the side," he told her, "and look at that window down there above the fire escape. You'll see a guy with a telescope or binoculars."

She moved to the window's edge. "My god!"

"The feds are checking us out this week. In a couple of days they'll move on to someone else, another Moratorium organizer."

"You'd think you were underground guerillas!" Beth said. Her voice shuttled between outrage and disbelief.

"Our phones are probably tapped though we don't know for sure," Frank told her. "When you call your man, here," (he put his hand on James' shoulder) "don't say anything intimate, unless you want to. And don't be surprised if James says something weird you don't understand. We may be planting misinformation."

He never imagined how much planning was needed for what they were trying to do.

They came together with no central person the leader, but by three weeks before the national Moratorium there were twenty of them who were meeting regularly, coordinating with one another, sharing their talents.

He was in charge of getting various speakers and arranging the events for the College of Arts and Letters. It sounded easy at first, but then he became aware of the intricacies of scheduling one event to coincide with another, arranging housing for out-of-town participants, obtaining permits for rooms and lecture halls, and providing adequate parking. None of them knew anything about publicity until two marketing majors from the business school saved them.

They learned as they went along, he wrote Beth, becoming resourceful as needed. They found out how to move the university's bureaucracy and how to raise funds.

They learned to rely on one another, to tell each other when something wasn't going to work, to thank and support each other. Stuffing informational mailers, they learned each other's life histories and shared all the good jokes going around campus.

They lived on Cokes, potato chips, and carry-out pizzas—barely slept as they got nearer to their target date.

They had to generate enough events to involve large numbers of people, but they had to limit themselves to what could be successful. Three days before Moratorium weekend, he called Beth, telling her his fears that what they'd planned wouldn't go over well.

In the fieldhouse there were so many people they were standing in the aisles, around and behind the bleachers, and in the areas in front of the closed concession stands. It was as though the university's basketball team was in the finals of a national tournament.

Tonight was the second of three days of activities. Yesterday the readings and lectures he organized were well attended, but the turnout tonight almost overwhelmed him.

He shook hands with his former professor, as John Oates went to the podium to preside. He thought back to the day the man had refused to sign his petition after class. What a long time ago that was!

Five speakers appeared, and then a middle-aged woman came to the mike, to talk about her son. In a strained voice, in inflection shaking with emotion, she told how her son had recently returned from Vietnam.

Missing, she said, was the smile her family had gotten accustomed to. Gone was the easy manner they had known for twenty years. Instead came the military-issue coffin with her son's body. Why, she asked the audience, did her son die? Was there a purpose to the war? What was it? Would it go on forever? When, when would the Congress listen, listen to them? The audience leaned toward her final appeal: "Bring home our boys, now, bring home our boys!" And then the whole of the great crowd rose with a simultaneous, resolute and staunch dignity to begin chanting: "Out of Vietnam, Out of Vietnam!" It was a full three minutes later that John Oates or anyone else was able to gain a commanding voice to tell the people of upcoming events of the following day.

Next day there were to be speeches in front of the Administration Building, after which crowds were to march to the city's business district, to join business and labor people against the war. Both groups would then proceed to the county courthouse where the County Clerk would officially receive petitions to be sent to Washington. After that there would be a rally on the state capitol grounds, and then a vigil there, during which all the names of the war dead would be read one at a time in front of a symbolic coffin. A bell would toll for each name as it was read.

Frank and he were in charge of directing and controlling the university marchers, about three thousand strong.

In the past weeks they had gotten members of the fraternity council to sign on as marshals along the route. Local ministers were also going to place themselves strategically among the crowd. But the heavy responsibility for keeping order was in the hands of the Vets for Peace group, which had met with the organizing committee two nights before.

One of the vets was on the walkie-talkie at the moment, reporting that the marchers were past Sixth Street, one of the places where they thought the marchers could be provoked into violence. There Sixth Street opened into a blind alley that could have held disrupters.

For the last two months on campus, gangs of them had been active, doing petty damage to property but threatening the Moratorium efforts. He and his fellow organizers knew the press was just waiting to show the weekend activities as the work of delinquents, anarchists, or wild socialists.

From the speakers' platform, ten minutes later, he and Frank saw the first of the massed marchers coming up the long street toward them.

They watched, satisfied, for ten minutes more. But then they heard the chants: "Che lives! Che lives!"

Frank was on the walkie-talkie faster than he was: "Jimmy," he crackled into it, "you've got a loose cannon, on my forty-five yardline near Henson's Shoe Store."

The walkie-talkie barked back: "We're already on our way there."

The student government president, to Frank's left, started to go give assistance, but he held him back, telling him to not feed the situation or TV people would head to the scene. Jimmy and his vets would handle everything.

The chant, which caught on for a brief time, died as the vets, with their armbands, moved in around the original chanters and quieted things down. A moment later the vets muscled a flailing figure out of the march area and around toward the back of a nearby building, toward a room set aside for such a purpose.

"It went well, didn't it, Frank?" he said half an hour later, after the formal presentation of the petition was made and the crowds were breaking up.

"Yes. Are you staying around for the reading of the names?"

"I'm coming back later for that."

On an impulse he walked from his observer's platform down to the building where the vets had taken their prisoner. One of them was coming out the door as he went in, and he held up a red flag for him to see. "Our agitator friend had this," the man said. "Sure as hell would have been a great news story for the military freaks in town."

"Probably would have made national news too. You guys did a great job. Thanks!"

He followed the man inside and found himself looking at Randy, behind a table, his legs up on a chair next to him. He was reading a magazine the vets had given him.

"Never thought of you as a kidnapper, James," he said jauntily. How long are you and your goons gonna keep me here?" His face changed expression, and he added meanly: "You sure know how to spoil somebody's fun."

That night he went to the capitol square to help dismantle the mini-stage where the names of the war dead were being read aloud over the microphone. As he walked from the campus and got close to where he was going, he could still hear the names being pronounced, after which someone tolled a bell.

It was raining, fittingly he thought, a dull relentless drizzle, as he walked up and stood next to a fellow organizer, named Jan, who reminded him of Rosa, back home.

"This was supposed to end an hour ago, wasn't it?" he said, as the reader of the names came to the end of the W's.

"There are more dead than we thought," came the answer.

They stood in the rain, barely speaking, for another half hour, and then they set to work. Yes, he repeated to himself, it had been a successful three days. But none of those whose names had been spoken over the microphone would know that.

"My turn to be exhausted," he was telling Beth over the phone. "It's the tension from wanting everything to go well, I guess."

For Beth it had been an easy week for a change. Homecoming at Braydon High School meant some canceled classes and regular days with light work loads. Students were decorating the gym, going to pep rallies, and working on parade floats.

At the parade through town, she told him, the American Legion contingent was small this year. Maybe even the hard core war supporters were losing their enthusiasm. She'd even seen one or two OUT OF VIETNAM bumpers stickers lately, in the conservative small community.

They talked about getting together at Thanksgiving but decided they'd go to Harris Point instead, at Christmas, when she'd have more time.

"You won't forget me till then, will you?" she joked.

"Don't be silly."

Three days later she sent him a letter, reeking of her perfume.

That same day, after her phone call, he and Frank were eating in the front window area of Warren's, when Randy walked by on the other side of the street. James pointed him out, reminding him of Randy's action the week before and his pelting the police during the Dow-Protest days.

"Ah yes," Frank said, "our local revolutionary. Che Guevara's disciple, Señor Castro's henchman, smuggled onto the U." He was enjoying the speculation, seeing its loony possibilities.

"Randy's politics are pretty anemic," he confirmed. "Mainly he does things to get attention. In high school as a senior it was shoplifting, and his dad was wealthy enough to get him off with a slap of the wrist when he got caught. Daddy Fahey actually bragged about the whole thing–thought it was clever."

Frank shook his head. "Pathetic. So where'd he get the red flag? He must have connections to the far left."

"Maybe so, maybe not."

It was during final exam week. He ran into Oates in the back stacks of the library, leafing through a scholarly journal, and he thanked him for presiding over the fieldhouse events. John told him in turn that the university had been well served by his Moratorium work. "And what's next?" he wanted to know, his eastern accent creeping through slightly. "Grad school, James?"

"Maybe. Graduation first, at least. I had to add another semester, what with all the anti-Vietnam work I've been doing."

"How sad for all of you," Oates commiserated. "I've talked to so many like you lately."

They circled back to the events of the Moratorium weekend, and Oates told him that so many successful protests had taken place nationally, it was only a matter of time till a massive pull-out from Vietnam would begin. "God help us, if it doesn't," he added.

He'd spent time at Beth's house in August. Now it was her turn to visit the Brandes household in Harris Point, after Christmas. "My mother likes you a lot," he was saying. They were driving to get a pizza after a movie, at the new theater complex at the mall.

"I'm not too much a big-city girl for her?"

"Not at all. For Wendy it's a big plus though, and my dad told me you're pretty."

"Pretty as in pretty radical, for him, if we ever had a real conversation, I bet."

"Actually, his saying that was okay, his way of telling me I haven't gone completely crazy. I'm still a standard male finding a good-looking woman to spend my life with."

"All these compliments are making me nervous," Beth said. "Your mother's like a lot of the moms I met at parent conferences in Braydon, sweet and solid, the rock of the community."

He turned off the main road onto a side street, letting the car come to a stop at the curb, a mile beyond. "I wanted to show you this," he said. Then he explained that the house belonged to parents of a high-school friend, Rosa—that her parents got the house only when the color barrier of segregated housing came down with civil rights law. "I come by here when I'm home," he said, "just to remind myself: Government made this house happen."

"One good thing by Uncle Sam," she agreed. "But there's all the other, the screwed up Defense Department mentality." She put his hand on his.

"I come here for that reason too," he admitted. Then he told her about Rosa's brother, Gerald, winning the purple heart but losing a leg. "I don't know how many times I come back here, literally and when I'm at school. I think how blacks and poor whites fight for us, as we go off to college with our deferments, to pontificate on the war's evil. Christ, while we're speaking out, they go through the real stuff!"

"It's not hypocrisy, if that's what you're thinking." Beth was rising to the intellectual challenge.

"That's exactly what I think at times." He'd never really been able to reconcile this dilemma in his mind, and he felt no less torn now.

"Your work—ours!—brings everybody home, blacks and poor people included," Beth said softly, after a minute.

"But it doesn't seem enough! Why Gerald Parson's leg and not mine?" He was three hundred sixty degrees round to guilt again.

"No more war, no legs lost for anyone,"she tried to reassure him. When she saw he wasn't convinced, she added, "As a woman, maybe I can't see this as you do. Sorry."

The next afternoon his mother was out to the hairdresser, and his dad was at work. Wendy was leading them down to the basement to his dad's workroom. "I found out by accident," she was telling them. "One day I was looking for a screwdriver upstairs. There wasn't one there in the junk drawer so I came down here."

Wendy led them into the six by eight room with its single overhead light. She pulled a covered cardboard box from under a workbench and removed the folded paper hiding its contents.

It was a box full of all the books written by President Nixon, during his long career in politics.

"Make sure you keep them in order, or he'll know we've been here," Wendy warned.

"So this is what he's been doing down here, immersing himself in this man's life! And we thought he was just putzing!"

"Eccentric to say the least," Beth commented.

"Look at this." Wendy led their glance to a small drawer labeled "Bolts." When she pulled it out, they saw a batch of "Nixon Now" and "Nixon—Agnew" political buttons.

"But he never wore a campaign button in his life!" James said, shaking his head with growing surprise.

"Mom wouldn't let him, remember? She always thought politics was distasteful."

Wendy added that there were about twenty to thirty buttons. She couldn't figure out if their dad bought them all at once or at random intervals. Probably at different times, she said, since there were different kinds of them. But that meant he must have been sneaking off to a campaign headquarters.

"Like some closet drunk hitting the liquor store?" he suggested, and they all shared a humorous moment over the image.

"Step back so I can open this," Wendy commanded. Then she swung back the door on the large tool cabinet on the wall behind them. When she opened it, they saw the poster covering the whole backside of the door. NIXON'S THE ONE it said under the glossy smile of the man who was so despised on campus.

"Damn, it's a shrine!" Beth exclaimed.

"And Nixon for a god!" he said back, pointing to the image of their commander-in-chief. "How appalling!"

On Campus, January–April 1970

It was teeth-clenching cold for two months. Beth had finished her student-teaching internship the week before classes began, and she was delighted to be back on campus, but they didn't go out to their old haunts as they wanted to do. The cold imprisoned them in their apartments and restricted their coming and goings to the classroom buildings, the student union and the libraries.

He manned the draft counseling tables as always, but now there was little need for his work. On campus there was a universal, raw defiance of anything military. All over, in every building, literature was posted on ways to avoid the draft, to create legal nightmares for the draft-board system, to claim conscientious-objector status, to flee to Canada if the obstruction failed.

The anti-Dow protestors received light sentences. Even at the state capitol–Frank called it the legislative country club—calls for withdrawal of troops were being heard. The war was being seen more and more as unwinnable.

He, Beth, Frank, all the students like them, waited to see what the president would do. Peace negotiations were going on in Paris, but most students saw them as a public relations ploy by the Nixon Administration.

More treachery seeped out slowly, in early February, in pictures, aerial reconnaissance photos, obtained in Europe and transmitted to U.S.

TV screens. Nixon was lobbing tens of thousands of bombs into North Vietnamese cities.

Frank and he watched, the night the story broke. The bombing targets were supposedly military installations exclusively, but civilian buildings having nothing to do with the war were being hit. Huge craters had been left all over North Vietnam, destroying the rice fields. Dikes constructed over five hundred years were being obliterated in seconds by B-52 raids on the landscape.

"This isn't true, is it," Frank wanted to know, "that we've dropped more bombs on that little scrap of a country than we dropped in all of World War II?"

"Is that a rhetorical question?" He thought his roommate was fending off his anger with high irony, a talent they all had down to a science by now. It was just one more form of psychic survival!

"No! For god's sake."

"Sorry. And the answer's yes, if you really want to know." James was amazed that his roommate, the resident cynic, still had some capacity for being astounded. Practically no one did anymore.

In Europe, reporters were saying, more and more people were comparing the U.S. action to the scorched earth policy of the Nazis during World War II.

The reporters were pressing the White House to respond, but the president was invisible and not making any comments through his aides. He seemed to be the Jekyll and Hyde his fiercest opponents painted him as.

They found they had no more energy. Instead they sank into a collective depression, aware that their efforts in the fall might actually have sent the president into a reflex of ego: They'd protested; he'd taken their rebellion as personal insult and rubbed their noses in his military options.

Even the hard-core faithful, the odd dozen who'd unbelievingly continued picketing Horton Hall in the icy days, dwindled away. The building stood there, unchallenged, silica grey against the skyline.

They lost control, neuroned away from normalcy.

Frank ate and ate more, gave up all athletic activity, gained ten pounds in a month.

Beth obsessed on a small item in the local paper. A former campus spy, a woman who'd been exposed by the anti-war groups, was suing her former employer, the FBI, for breach of contract. She'd been guaranteed two years' work, she said, but been exposed after one, so her salary was terminated. The woman was affronted and had a lawyer. Beth carried the story around, told everyone about it, roared about it, roared continuously, did nothing but talk about it—until he had to tell her that she was telling everyone what she'd already told them, sometimes twice. She lapsed into a three-day silence then and only came back to herself after a whole weekend of sleep.

James buried himself in a news story from Maryland, which he videotaped. Whales, five disoriented ones, had beached themselves in an area where they couldn't be reached by heavy equipment. Now they were dying, slowly hour by hour, their flesh about to rot, their smell about to be carried inland with the winds.

He ran the videotape over and over, and taped follow-up stories, as he missed classes for two days. Beth, coming off her own depression, gave him time and space. At the end of the second day she asked him what he was seeing, trying to discover. "They'll die," she told him. "You can't prevent it."

"I just want them to find out," he whispered.

"Find out what?"

"Well, it's a strange hope, but I want the smell to find its way to Washington, to, uh…them."

"Them? I don't understand, Love."

"I'm not sure I do either. But maybe they'll see."

"The president?"

"Yes. He has to see this as a sign."

"An act of god, you mean?"

"No. Well, maybe, yes."

"But how will your watching make that happen?"

"I don't know," he admitted feebly, as he rewound the tape, not looking at her. When he pressed the Forward button, one of the whales, in closeup, heaved an extruded breath as its visible eye lidded over.

His mother wrote, repeating how much they liked Beth when he brought her home at Christmas. His father was better these days since Doctor Nelson had him on tranquilizers, and she appreciated James' not bringing up his views on the war over the holidays. She knew it was hard for him to keep quiet.

Did he have any plans for the future yet? she wanted to know.

Was there any future for any of them? he'd begun to ask himself. They would graduate perhaps, but then they would be called to fight and kill to satisfy the whims of a small pocket of ego-maniacal men in Washington, for whom war policy was numbers, abstractions, and twisted ideology. They gave people like him choices, to play the charade of representative government, or to choose exile as a penalty for having a human conscience. They'd driven them to unheard ways of thinking and acting. Last week Beth's former roommate, Anne, reintroduced herself to everyone as Magenta Magdalene, acid queen, who heard from god through the hiccups of a street peddler. She was holding nightly seances and gathering a rabid following.

He didn't know what to write his mother. In the end he jotted a note saying that he'd only been thinking of finishing the following year.

Spring arrived as climatic joke, thaw and blizzard, sunlight and sleet. In early April it rained a whole week, then summer was there, humid, sticky. Buds bloomed in a day and fell.

Beth went off to job interviews at spring break while he stayed on campus, toying at neglected studies. She came back, having been hired in a school district close to the one where she student-taught. She was happy being back, seeing him again, but she was brought back to the political realities that were part of the campus. "I should be happy," she told him. "I'm about to graduate, I've got a job, and I'm moving on in life. So why am I gloomy?"

The president reemerged, his bloated jowls and sinister eyebrows accented in the camera close-up.

Two weeks before final exams his announcement came, that as commander-in-chief he was sending U.S. troops into Cambodia, to wipe out supply dumps being used there by the north Vietnamese.

"He's actually expanding the war!" Frank came running into the apartment with the news. "Risking Chinese involvement! There's going to be an all-campus strike of classes. People are over in the student union, organizing it!"

The next morning pickets were in front of every classroom building, and only about half the students were attending classes, many of which weren't being held because professors themselves were refusing to teach. Huge rallies were planned for noon, but large crowds were already gathering spontaneously at various places. Two or three people would shout "Shut it down! Shut it down!" and the chant would grow till it sounded like a pep rally. By eleven o'clock police cars were patrolling the streets, their windows taped to prevent glass from shattering. Inside, the helmeted faces looked worried.

In the afternoon, after the rallies, TV programming was interrupted to report that National Guard troops had fired on and killed four students in a rally at Kent State University in Ohio. Frank, Beth, and he watched horrified at seeing students falling in front of an advancing column of troops. The recorded gunfire pop-popped, and then the students were lying there, their blood seemingly coming from out of the ground, from springs, rather than from their bodies.

Frank pounded the table: "Jesus! who gave them the ammunition, the order to fire?"

They went outside to the main part of the campus, just in time to hear the first sirens and to smell the tear gas. People were running toward them wildly, holding handkerchiefs over their noses to deaden the effects. The chanting continued but from pockets between buildings, out of chemical range.

By midnight the four-mile square university area was wreathed in a sticky, vaporous mist that hung like fog beneath the street lights. Store windows in the campus's shopping area were being trashed, and masses of students were roaming the pavements, on the alert for cruising squad cars, which would roar to a stop, emit someone who would shoot off a canister and slip rapidly back inside. As the cars drove off, they would be pelted with glass bottles and other debris.

When he and Frank got back to the apartment at two, they fell exhausted on their beds, but the phone got him to his feet again.

It was Dean Hart, from the university's administration, whom he'd worked with during the Moratorium events. "James," the man's voice said hoarsely, "I'm calling to ask you to do something. We need to try to cool what's going on."

He thought a minute, trying to collect his thoughts. He remembered liking the man for his honesty. "I'm sorry," he answered. "This thing is really bigger than the university community."

"I know that," he heard. "But this rioting doesn't seem to get us anywhere."

"Has anything else gotten us anywhere, Dean Hart? It's pretty obvious what the president thinks of us, the so-called people."

"But what should we do here, James? What would you do if you were in the chancellor's shoes?"

"Shut the school down for the year." He was a little surprised at how fast he responded, but it was the instant right answer.

"What about those who want to attend classes? Don't we owe them something?"

"We owe them a national government," he said, starting to tremble uncontrollably from fatigue and long-standing fury, "that won't make us all go insane."

"A little bird is telling me," Randy said. He looked like hell, having been up all night squaring off against whatever authorities he could find to aggravate or lambast. But his voice still had a high-pitched snarl to it.

They were having breakfast at Warren's, having found each other by accident on the street. This morning Warren's windows were ply-wooded up. Normally customers like them in the front booths would be looking out onto passing student traffic.

"What's the bird telling you?"

"Something big's about to happen."

"Stop being coy, Randy."

"Your ears are so deaf you oughtta be eighty."

"That's all you're going to tell me?" He felt annoyed but also spell-bound, the way he and his classmates often were back in high school. Randy hadn't lost that charisma of suspenseful feistiness that made him so popular there.

"Everybody in town but you knows. Telling you would be a waste of time."

"Then what does everybody know?"

Randy's expression curled into more mocking haughtiness. "Maybe I'll tell you the kind of bird."

James found his ire stirring again, but he tried to put things in some perspective: "Look, I know we spoiled your fun at the Moratorium, but—" He thought how odd the choice of word was: *fun*! But that was exactly how Randy saw the Moratorium.

"Hey, friends forgive, buddy! Forgive and forget!"

James let himself calm down as he spread raspberry jelly on his piece of toast. Should he ask another question on his mind? Why should he, if he knew the answer? But a nagging need to know rapped at the back of his head. "What do you find so fascinating about Che Guevara?" he said. In his mind was the real question: *Do you know who this guy is?*

"Who?"

"Che Guevara. He's the guy whose name you were chanting at the Moratorium rally that day. The Cuban communist." *So you don't know!*

Randy, weary as he was, could have tried to hide his ignorance. Instead, he let conversation skitter off: "I met one of those the other day, an agitator from Philadelphia." He poured some milk into his coffee. "I tried to tell him about Harris Point, about how people live there. The jerk had no idea." Then he held up his cup: "Cheers, ol' buddy! Entertaining days, hey? Maybe we'll have some real excitement tonight."

For the next day and a half TV reports showed campus rioting all over the U.S. On their own streets the three of them watched the police and national guard play hit and run with the students. By night the students would put up barricades of trash barrels and broken furniture, which would be removed during the day by street crews.

After dark the barricades would be up again. Trucks holding combat-ready personnel would come into an area and clear it of clustered rioters, who would then reappear a block away, which would start another cycle of troops getting into trucks, moving, and clearing still another sector.

In the main housing area of the campus so much tear gas had been set off, students were moving elsewhere to sleep, to friends' housing farther from the university's center.

Mid-day, Frank and he saw a young student, a skinny and freckled stick of a guy, get caught after throwing a beer bottle at a squad car. The guardsman who collared the student was proceeding to thrash him on his neck with a nightstick, and Frank ran up to the scene within ten yards of the clubbing, yelling "Stop it! Stop it, Please!" James raced after his roommate, to pull him back, as the student was dragged to a doorway opening and let recover momentarily. The guardsman, removing his helmet, looked as dazed as his victim.

An hour later he was back at the apartment where he found a note taped to the door, in Frank's handwriting: CALL YOUR SISTER.

On the phone he plunged right into conversation, asking her what was going on at the small private college she was attending. He wasn't surprised that classes there were being canceled too. Did she think that—?

But then Wendy was hesitating in a way that told him he should stop talking.

"James," he heard her say, "is Beth there?"

"No, why?"

"Find her as soon as you can. You'll need her with you." His sister's voice held a shaky nervousness.

"Why, Wen?"

"It's—Mom called me this morning. Oh, James, it's Howard. He was killed in action. Mom wanted me to call you, so I could—"

His mind groped: "There's no mistake or anything?" He could feel his thoughts trying to buy time before the crush of grief hit. Maybe a subtle question would fend away its impact although he knew better.

"No, there's no mistake."

"No, I know that. It was stupid to ask."

"He'll be home on Thursday. I mean—I'm sorry."

"I know what you mean. Don't apologize."

"The funeral's Saturday. His folks are taking it very hard. The problem is, there wasn't much of him to ship home. He stepped on a mine. God, I really shouldn't be telling you all this, should I? It's not important how he died."

"I'll be there," he said, and he realized how little strength his voice had. Memories of his high school friend were starting to make themselves known, and the mix of hot-core anger, disbelief, and wrenching sadness was forming. "Saturday?"

"Yes. Go find Beth. You'll need her."

They rode in one of the last cars, his mother and father and himself, and another woman, a sister of Mrs. Parker, who'd flown in from South Dakota the day before. His mother and the woman talked of their home towns, his father drove, and he looked out the window. He felt numb as though he were no longer capable of sensing touch, yet he knew very well that he was making contact with things—he could feel ridges in the car's upholstery, the smoothness of the stainless steel door handle, the lint on his suit.

They wound their way up a series of gravel paths between grave plots, memorial statues, and headstones. A groundskeeper paused to look at them, as a man in the car ahead pointed to his right, indicating something of importance to the people he was riding with.

He was thinking of a story he read one time. In it was a scene much like the one he was about to witness. But in the story as the coffin was lowered into the ground, a large monarch butterfly came and sat on it for a split second. After that it rose as if carrying the spirit of the dead person with it, heavenward.

He didn't think anything like that would happen now, and he wondered what Howard thought about an afterlife. But there was no way of knowing, and he felt himself dogged instead by a silly image, Howard standing on the stage of the high school auditorium, forgetting his meager three lines, in the last act of the senior play. Why was he remembering that? Because Howard hadn't wanted to be in the play at all? Yes. *You always did what others wanted, How.*

The car stopped, its doors opened.

"James?" his father said, leaning his head back inside. "You getting out?"

He got out and heard his mother say to the other woman, softly so that he wouldn't hear, that he was taking Howard's death very hard. He was moody and untalkative from the moment he got home.

They all followed the casket and Howard's family to the burial site, where the minister would perform the rest of the ritual. He thought he must have looked at least as terrible as Jennifer, Howard's girlfriend, who was making the reluctant voyage to Howard's final internment, her feet dragging anchor with each step. He wasn't sure she could make the slight grade they were walking up.

He was conscious of the minister's voice, rising and falling in the speaking pattern of people of the cloth. Then he heard the man say that a color guard would fire a twenty-one gun salute, up there, there on the hill in the distance, where a small group of American Legion officers stood.

As the guns began firing, he found himself turning away and striking off in an oblique direction, toward the city, as his anger came back. *Why let guns honor someone killed in some gun-filled place? Obscenity piled on obscenity*! *Let Howard have peace*, he vowed.

He wanted nothing to do with anyone right now. He saw his mother looking at him quizzically as she leaned slightly toward his dad, who was standing in a rigid military salute. Over his shoulder he gave a half-hearted wave to her, to let her know he'd be okay on his own.

When he'd gone forty yards, he saw another figure isolated from the crowd, watching the ceremony from a distance.

The person came out from the shade of an oak tree, his hands on his hips, as though he were someone in authority pronouncing judgment. He took off his sunglasses before speaking. "We shoulda stopped him, James," Randy said, gesturing back toward the canopied grave site. "He was too stupid to know what he was getting into."

"Let's go somewhere and talk," he finished, which they did, in a conversation whose words would alter everything, beyond any boundary of James' hopelessly miniscule imagination.

On Campus and In the Upper Midwest, Late May 1970

They came hustling down the street toward him, in the running car, and in sun glasses in the pre-dawn darkness they looked funny, but really everything about what they were doing was sobering serious, he reminded himself.

"Go! Move it!" Randy said, as he and the man named Gates plunged into the car pell-mell. Gates had trouble doing so, since his tall frame didn't fit easily into the back seat.

"Great! Not a soul saw us!" Randy went on, slapping his leg in self-congratulation. "Get this sucker going, James! Whooeee!"

In the ensuing minutes James sped them through downtown streets toward the city's edge, getting them out of town quickly but quietly.

"How much time till detonation?" This to Gates, behind him.

Gates' illuminated watch made a faint zephyr of light in the backseat. "Eight minutes, twenty seconds. No, twenty-four." The words came deliberately, Gates reinforcing an impression of careful precision he'd made on the only other occasion James had been with him. That was the night before last when they'd set the final plans for the fire-bombing of Horton Hall.

"No problem ditching the van?" he inquired. *I need assurance.*

"Easy as pie. Right, Gates?" Answering, gleeful almost, Randy reached over to hit the On button of the Mercury's radio, and in a second it was pumping rock at high volume, filling the interior with vibrating waves.

Gates' face, though, suddenly appeared over the seat. "Turn it down," he ordered. "We don't want to call attention to ourselves."

Four traffic lights and three miles later, at the city's edge as he got to a highway, James thought he saw something like a flash in the rear-view mirror. Then the flash seemed to be followed by a crruumphing explosion, something like a Fourth of July skyrocket. "Jesus!" he said. "That wasn't us, was it?"

"Are you kidding?" Randy jeered.

"What was it then?"

"Who the hell knows?"

He took Randy at his word—he had to—but he felt uneasy. Gates, behind him, was saying nothing, and, like him or not, Gates gave off confidence and calm.

Earlier, waiting in the car for Gates and Randy to appear, he'd relived the agitation of previous days.

Back on campus after Howard's funeral, he'd found far fewer students there, and Frank, about to leave for home for the summer, said all remaining semester classes and exams were canceled. University administrators were telling faculty to give grades as best as they could, on whatever criteria seemed reasonable. Some of the teaching assistants were giving all A's as a form of further protest.

"James?"

"Pardon?"

"Are you hearing me at all?"

"Mmnn." Staring out the apartment window.

Frank shifted thoughts, seeing he was dealing with a listener with a short attention span. "Those guys who are sub-letting want to move in next week."

"Mmnn."

"I said—" Frank bobbed his face in front of him, forcing eye contact.

"I heard you." Eyes finally focused on his caring roommate.

"Look, should I score some Valium for you? You look wired."

"I am."

"You're not going to do anything silly, are you? What is I mean is, the National Guard's still on the streets, but they're pulling out."

Rather than follow Frank's train of thought, he went off on one of his own. "Do you know what I saw this morning, outside the Greyhound station?"

Frank held his arms open, anticipating, grateful for James' participation in the conversation at long last, no matter that his talk jumped all over like a flying electrical wire in a storm.

"You'll think I'm making this up, but I'm not, and the only thing I've been on is aspirin. You know my leeriness about drugs."

"Yes, go on."

"Anyway, I'm crossing the street near the bus station, not crossing but waiting, and one of those parking-meter jeeps pulls up to turn in front of me. It gets tied up in traffic, which lets me see inside, and I look in and see this weird thing on the shift counsel. A human skull! A model of one but a skull just the same."

"James, come on. Look, I'll get you the Valium."

"No, I saw this!"

"Sure!" Frank had him fixed in direct eye contact again, but he was a wearing a doubtful look.

"Frank, I'm not lying!"

"But the jeep was moving."

"No, stuck in traffic, so I get a second look, and it's what I think it is, and the driver, a woman about thirty, sees me looking at it, and..."

"Damn, you're not kidding!"

"...and she sees me with my mouth open, looking at the thing, confused. So she smiles at me, pats the skull's top like the thing's a pet or something. Then she smiles again before she drives away."

With Beth things were still strained but improving. He wasn't using her presence to feed his anger, even though she was still wary of that side of him, the side she'd only recently discovered. They talked of an earlier time, two years before, when student radicals had brought a twelve-foot high cake to the mall in front of the library. HAPPY BIRTHDAY, VIETNAM WAR the cake's lettering read on one side. On the other was SIX YEARS OLD. OUR BABY.

"Remember our reactions to that?" Beth reminisced. "About whether we should eat any of the cake or not?"

"Couldn't let the food go to waste, but we couldn't celebrate the war going on either. What a coup that was, a real conscience stirrer."

"If you ate, you gagged. If you didn't you felt wasteful."

He brought them out of their nostalgia. "It all seemed so radical then, but now it seems so tame." His words had wistful tones.

Beth edged the discussion back toward *their* past. "You seem a little better today, less distracted and more—what?—*here*, I guess. True?"

"I think I have to do something," he said, not answering directly. "Will you be here two days from now, before you leave for Ryan's Park?"

"Yes. What are you going to do?" Beth was trying not to pry, he could tell, for fear of upsetting him.

"Something for Randy, that guy I knew in high school."

"I thought you didn't like him."

He evaded again, telling her he loved her still and wanted to marry her. He thought maybe he'd visit her at home in a couple of weeks.

"I thought you were going back to that summer camp, next week."

No, he told her, he'd let the deadline pass for taking the job. And when she assumed that meant he was going to summer school, he said he hadn't applied for that either.

"Not like you, James,"she said, both pitying and perplexed.

They were going to make love, but as soon as she was out of her jeans he was horrified. Her whole outside left thigh was a jaundiced yellow and anemic purple, the bruise eighteen to twenty inches long. "God, what happened to you?" He felt if he touched her she'd be in instant pain.

"It's actually much better now,"she said, pulling him toward her. "Just a little sore."

She told him how it happened, how she had gone into the Unitarian church on the campus's main street, during the worst of the chaos. The church was being used by the students as a makeshift infirmary, and she'd gone there to help, and had in fact given aid for three hours. Then, coming out on the street again, after dark, in the tear-gas lemon light, she'd fallen/skidded/slid down a dozen steps because at the top of them was shattered glass. There was smashed glass everywhere on campus, every place where there was a window to be trashed by rioters. You couldn't walk the streets; you skated over them, as though it was winter after an ice-storm. She should have seen the glass, Beth said, but she hadn't, and she'd flown off the upper landing.

"Never mind that now," she said. "Come lie down next to me."

He felt the dislocation then, his mind taking him away, into rage and then toward an embering but unfocused determination. The Washington people had done this too, to her. Oh, he knew it was irrational, his thinking that way, but he could see too in a bizarre way that he was right. "I'm sorry," he said. "I've got to go," and he saw her trying to bring him back.

"We can just talk if you like—not do this." She gestured toward the bedclothes she was sitting on. Confused, helpless.

"No." For a moment he thought he'd say yes and return to her side, but then he decided, because Howard was behind him, saying "*You need to act*," and then Howard's voice was submerged in the image of Beth's thigh, multicolored. Sound to color transitions. Dead voices to live ones. No sense. "I'll see you in two days." His hand was on the doorknob, and it wasn't very light in the apartment but light enough for him to see the moist splotch on her cheek. "I'll be all right," he assured her, turning away.

They stopped to change drivers. When they got back onto the highway, Gates was behind the wheel, intensely bunched into the seat, eyeing forward as though sighting a rifle. He drove like a machine, steady and concentrated.

Gates had to be six feet six, but if he was maximum in height, he was also a minimalist with words, although his speech was precise, elegant almost, in its simplicity. He was also older than Randy and him, about twenty-five, James guessed.

He'd met Gates two nights before, when the three of them went over the plans. He tried to be friendly, but Gates was circumspect or offish, he couldn't tell which. Randy told him Gates was a journalism major, but he didn't look like a student, maybe because of his age.

After they separated that night he realized he didn't know Gates's first name. He thought he heard Randy use "Steve" once, to address him, but he wasn't sure.

The radio! At last a news report, the first they'd heard! Reporters were saying that a large bomb had gone off on the university campus within the hour, and more reports would follow in half an hour. At the moment everything was chaotic, but there had been tremendous devastation to the army math research facility on campus.

Randy was animated again, but in the back seat James suddenly felt very nervous. The bomb had to be much larger than the one Gates described, when they all went over final details.

They had three more hours to go that day, to a place Randy had rented months before, a small farmhouse that had a garage with a second car, one Randy and Gates would use to get to Canada. They would spend the night at the house, and then Gates or Randy would drive him to a bus station in the nearest town, while he would head back to campus, and then Harris Point probably, to resume something like normal summer life.

Normal life. Two weeks before, he never would have thought of himself as a getaway man for people setting fire to a government facility. But that was before Kent State, and Howard's funeral, the coupled events that sent him into those days of nervous depression when he barely slept, hardly ate.

They met together just once, the three of them, as Randy explained that Gates would set the fire, Randy would act as lookout, and James would be ready a block away from Horton Hall, in the running car. He would just be a driver, and he would actually feel better because he'd be taking action, Randy said, doing something instead of giving into further moroseness.

Everything seemed okay and logical then, he thought, and things seemed to have gone according to plan except for the size of the bomb.

When they stopped for gas, at eight, at a run-down station, the three of them got out to stretch their legs. Gates and Randy went inside, while he stayed by the car, chatting with the attendant about the weather. Later the attendant went inside, and he saw Randy pull out his wallet and pay the man, after which the three of them stood there talking for a moment.

He thought he saw Randy's face wince visibly, just for a split second, although he couldn't trust his observations. Gates had his back turned, too, so there was no way to cross-reference. But then when Gates and Randy got outside again alone, the two remained at the door conversing, glancing his way, he thought, in an uneasy manner.

They came back to the car.

"What's up?" he asked quietly.

Randy tossed him the car keys. "You're driving again. That's what's up." But his mood was too jaunty to seem natural.

"I don't mean that," he said, pressing the point.

"What're you talking about?" Randy asked.

"You seemed to react to something the attendant told you. I was watching you in the window."

Randy tried to show surprise, he thought: "Gates, did I do something strange in there?" When Gates shook his head, he fell into his usual smug confidence. "There's your answer," he said, almost mockingly. His body language seemed forced, however.

They got back in the car and took off again with him behind the wheel. It felt good to drive once more, to be able to release his tension into the mechanics of maneuvering down the highway.

But the bombing squeezed into his mind, so he reached over to the radio to get more news. Just as quickly, though, Randy, who was drowsing next to him, stirred and turned it off immediately. "Gates is asleep," he said. "He gets ticked off if somebody wakes him."

How does Randy know that? He wondered more, too, about just who Gates was. The man constantly seemed to be picking at his fingernails, either from vanity or fidgetiness. If it was the latter, he thought, what was its source?

Well, he concluded, after tomorrow, when he was back on campus, he wouldn't have to care about the answer, or about Gates at all. He drove on, the white line arrowing him down the concrete miles, and the car, Randy's powerful V8, running superbly.

Later in a small town Randy got pulled over for speeding.

As the town cop came to a stop behind them, Randy looked to Gates, in the front seat beside him. "Let's run for it," he said. "When the guy gets out of his car, I'll burn us outta here."

Gates immediately assumed a commanding tone. "Don't be silly. It's a traffic ticket, for god's sake. Don't lose your cool."

"He's only a local! A sheriff!"

"Shut up. Here he comes."

When the man came to the window and asked for Randy's license, Randy started to become antagonistic, demanding to know why he was being pulled over.

"Let's just see your license first," the man said. He was soft-spoken for a policeman, but from the back seat James could see that he wasn't going to be timid for long, if Randy acted this way.

"I wasn't speeding," he said grudgingly, tendering up his license.

"You were seven over," the policeman replied. "How about all of you stepping out of the car for a minute? And I'll need to see everyone's license."

Randy was about to protest, but Gates interrupted: "Sure, officer. We need to get the kinks out anyway."

They all got out, and he saw Gates move immediately toward Randy, to take charge of the situation if the cop started addressing him again. He was impressed with Gates's smoothness and assurance.

The cop looked in the front seat, pulled his head back out, and opened the back door. "Mind opening the trunk?" he asked.

Randy was on the verge of taking on the man again, but Gates once more preempted any move. He put his hand on Randy's shoulder and led the officer to the back of the car. Opening the trunk, he gazed around and commented: "Nice little town here, reminds me of where I grew up, in Ohio."

The cop softened. "Well, we like it here. Which part of Ohio?" He was writing their names on a clipboard.

"Outside Canton. Town with three bars and three churches. An even stand-off."

The cop smiled. "Pretty much like here. You all on a trip? Going fishing?" He was eyeing the fishing tackle they'd put there as cover.

"After some bass," Gates replied.

"Water'll still be cold this time of year," the cop said. He paused a minute, and walked over to Randy, standing alone, leaning against the front fender, arms crossed. "Okay, I'm going to give you a warning ticket this time. You take it easy when you go through places like this, understand? Kids run out in the streets without thinking."

He saw Randy start to sneer, but Gates was there again, right at the cop's side, distracting him: "Thanks," he said. "That's nice of you. We'll drive slower." He took Randy's keys, motioned the two of them, Randy and him, into the car, chatted with the cop a bit more, and then waited patiently while the man went round and gave Randy the warning ticket.

Still smiling his obedient-citizen smile as they drove away, Gates said to Randy under his breath: "Listen, you jerkhead, you want a war with somebody, you do it by yourself. You almost screwed us for life."

"Goddamn John Law!" Randy started to say, but Gates cut him off.

"Shut it up!" His voice rose as his jaw set in furious anger. "Just shut it up, Stupid!"

They debated what to do, go directly on to the farm house Randy had rented or drive west, stay there and then return after a few days.

"I don't understand what danger we're in," James told his companions. "Why don't we stay with the original plan?"

"It's probably nothing," Gates said, shrugging his shoulders. "I was just thinking they'd expect us to head north. If we went west.... No, let's do what you say, go to the farmhouse. But let's stay there a couple of days, not take off right away."

"You'll drive me to the town with the bus station, though, right? Tomorrow, as planned?"

"Probably." Randy was studying the county map on his lap.

"Is there something you're not telling me? Something I should know?" He was almost afraid to ask the question, since questions usually brought answers.

Randy put the map down and craned his neck around to face him as he stretched his left leg in the back seat. "It wasn't a firebomb," he said.

"What?"

"The bomb that went off as we hit the city limits. We got the whole building." Randy's sentence started in seriousness, but as he neared its end, his familiar gloating expression reappeared.

"Good god! If I'd known you were going to do that–!"

"We'll never get caught. Don't sweat it!"

"But a regular bomb?"

"We called the police, and told them to evacuate the building." Gates, driving once more, didn't take his eyes from the road as he spoke.

"Gates isn't a student," Randy went on. "He's a demolitions expert." He waited a moment and then relished another fact: "The army taught him. In Vietnam."

Good god!

It was noon when they drove into a grove of oak trees next to a farmhouse, after which they swung the Mercury into an adjacent barn and closed the door. There, waiting, was the Chevy wagon they would use, to get him to the bus station and the other two to Canada—Canada, not a pure sanctuary but a safer place these days. How many young people had made peace with themselves there rather than submit to the madness they'd seen for six or seven years!

In the small farmhouse, full of dust and spiders, there was no electricity or plumbing. In the yard, under the largest tree, was a pump from which they could draw water.

Randy had rented the place in October, convincing the farmer-owner he wanted it as a hunting base. The guy, Randy told them, was only a farmer in name, his work taking place in the local bars and at his brother's trailer in town, where he hefted a whiskey bottle to his lips.

He found the bucket to bring the water in. It was already hot, for late May, and the three of them felt the bracing cold of the liquid from the well. Gates took a huge ladle-full, went back for seconds and then sprawled out on one of the dirty beds in the room adjoining the linoleum floored kitchen.

He wondered what kind of pills Gates took, during his second trip to the water bucket. After he was sure the man was sound asleep, he checked. Aspirin, he found out, when he checked the empty container in the wastebasket beneath the sink.

Gates took five of them, he knew, since he counted, out of Gates's direct line of vision. But why so many?

Randy fell asleep too, but James was still too keyed up. There were too many questions, too many wild conjurings in his head. Gates. Not a student, Randy finally admitted, but a demolitions expert who knew how to construct bombs, which he'd apparently done in this case.

Randy's assessment: "We got the whole place." *Literally true or just Randy's typical bragging? He meant the building's contents, surely.* But on the edge of the city, the car had shuddered when that skyrocket sound blasted the morning sky.

Maybe he was an accessory to something big, monstrous. His stomach clenched.

Randy hadn't leveled with him, most likely, and why should he be surprised at that? But he ached over his own naivete. Trust Randy? *So stupid of you, James. Foolish!*

He went outside, to stretch out in the tall grass under the oak trees, where he hoped to find some evenness of mood by thinking of Beth, but maybe there'd be nothing left of their relationship, he had to consider. *God knows I don't deserve her giving me any more sympathy.*

After Cambodia and before Howard's death he was already changing, and poor Beth soothed, sympathized, stroked. Tried to get him to talk, nursed his moods, attempted to reason. In return he slunk into a sullen shell or paradoxically lashed at things and let his anger explode, sometimes at her. Needing her, he told her to go away. At least he had the decency to spare her more hurt.

But she stayed with him until she, too, saw that he had to come to his own reckoning. "I'm fueling your hostility," she told him. "You and I both know it, and neither of us knows why, but it's silly for me to be around you." She was dead-center correct about that.

When he got back to her tomorrow, he wanted to believe, they'd be the Beth and James they were for almost two years. There were such reserves of warmth, courtesy, and care between them, they'd glue together everything shattered.

He wondered when, if at all, he'd tell her about his participation in this thing he was doing against their heinous government. A couple of years after they were married? Maybe never? She'd be dumbfounded, but she'd understand in time if he did tell. Probably the whole era would end soon, and the harshness of the time would dim, then fade. But how could it? There seemed to be no end of the mindlessness.

"I'll see you tomorrow," he said now to the image of Beth in his mind. *"It will all be good again, and we'll love as we once did."*

He drifted off. When he woke, he left the grove of oak trees and headed for the barn. In the back window ledge of the car was a book he'd left there, and he thought he'd begin reading it. Tomorrow on the bus, he'd finish it.

The barn smelled sour, and the light wasn't good, but he found the book easily. Getting out of the Mercury, though, he saw that the key was in the ignition, so he slipped into the driver's seat, settling there. *The radio*, he thought. *We haven't had it on since this morning.* He flipped the button on, saw the light suffuse the panel, and turned to a station.

For a couple of minutes he sat listening to the music, not a song he recognized, but a soothing ballad anyway. He could put his head back on the seat and be relaxed by it. The little throbs of tension he felt all day vanished from his temples.

He was pleasantly calmed, and then the news came on.

"Good evening," the announcer said. "As of this hour there are no leads in the bombing of a state university building last night. That blast, which gutted the inside of the six-storey army math research facility, claimed the life of thirty-four-year old physicist, Eric Forman. The father of two young daughters, his body was not found until this morning, when police were searching through the piles of rubble."

"Jesus!" he shouted, running from the barn. "My god!" He raced toward the porch, in front of which Randy was tending a twigs-and-sticks fire, on top of which he was cooking canned spaghetti.

"Lis—Listen! We killed somebody! On the car radio!" He was panting and trying to get his thoughts and words coordinated. "This morning in the rubble—they found a body! Two sons! No, daughters! He had a family. He's dead now! We've got to—"

He heard Gates come up behind him and to his left, so he turned to tell him too. But Gates was talking to him instead, coolly, levelly: "We know about it. I'm sorry."

"But we killed someone!"

Randy's voice was unruffled too. "We knew about it this morning. Big fucking deal."

"You should have told me!" he protested. Arms waving wildly.

Gates answered. "We knew you'd be like this. You'd have given us away, with that small-town cop."

"But there's someone dead now!"he began again. "You told me no one would be in the building."

"For chrissake, it was an accident!" Randy shouted. "You think we wanted the guy there? We even called the cops with a warning."

"Which didn't work!"

Randy was still impatient with him. "Stop walking around like a trapped animal."

He found himself trying to do something with his flailing upper limbs, to shake the dread out of them. "I just can't believe it! That man, he's really dead!"

Gates came over to him, putting his hand on his forearm. "We didn't want it to happen," he said. "Have some food and try to get some sleep. In the morning we'll decide what to do."

When the early morning sun came up onto the ridge, he was awake there, sitting up with his legs crossed Indian fashion, sitting in a musty blanket he'd brought outside with him. A crow was nagging him ruthlessly from a poplar tree, and his eyes simmered around the edges. He felt nauseous with exhaustion and at the same time ravenous. He was strangely hungry for bacon.

He heard Randy and Gates talking. A while later Randy came out to him. "We're going to lie low today," he said. "The latest news reports say someone spotted the Mercury. There's a reward of ten thousand for any information."

"What time is it?" he asked. "I've been awake most of the night."

Randy ignored the last comment. "Six," he answered.

"I suppose there's no point in my heading back by bus today, like we originally planned."

Randy seemed bored with his question. "Gates doesn't think so. It all depends on that puke of a cop who got our names. If he doesn't make a connection, you can go back. But you better stay with us till we know more."

It was terrible just waiting around, letting his mind dwell on things.

He went to Gates and asked if he thought it would be a good idea to call Beth, since she was expecting him the next day. Wouldn't it seem suspicious if he didn't make contact?

Gates told him he'd think about it, which he did for an hour. When he came back, he was working over one of his cuticles with that small penknife he always seemed to have out.

"Calling's probably not a good idea," he said. "The phone company tells you they don't keep records, but they can trace every call made by everybody. They could work back through your fiancee's records.

"But I'm not a suspect."

Gates was tight-lipped. "True. I guess."

The man's laconic replies set him on edge. "Is there anything else you and Randy haven't told me?"

Gates looked at him squarely. "No, truth told." Then he revealed a slightly warm side he hadn't shown before. "I'm sorry things worked out as they did for you. I still think we can get you back to campus okay. Hang in there."

Gates started to stroll off, but he called him back. "Can I ask," he said, "why you know that stuff about the phone company being able to trace calls? I mean, are you a criminal, that you know things like that?"

Gates let himself snicker a little. "Nothing so dramatic as that, I'm afraid. An army buddy from Nam told me that phone stuff. He worked for the phone company."

"Do you have a first name?"

The pocket knife was out again, and Gates' eye focused on another cuticle. "Steve," he said quietly. Then he looked up. "Is that "Siddhartha" you're reading?"

"Trying to. I can't keep my mind on anything. I still keep being yanked back to Horton Hall, to what we did."

"Not a bad book," Gates said elliptically. "I'm running low on aspirin. As you know. Got any?"

"No. I'm sorry. I didn't mean to spy on you." *How did he know? Eyes in the back of his head?*

"A little spying never hurts now and then," Gates said matter-of-factly. "Good skills to have in fact, say at times like this."

"I suppose," he said dejectedly.

"Try to get some rest," Gates urged. "We may have to get to town later. Can't have your eyeballs looking like that."

In the middle of the afternoon he fell into twitchy sleep. But coming out of it, he had a dream. He was in a city park, a distance away from a woman and her two daughters, as the woman pushed each of them alternately in their separate swings. She was a plain individual, her hair curly on one side but flat and cowlicky on the other near the back. There was a sweetness to her face, though, from a delicate fragility in the cheeks, although the fragility was also mirrored in a slump of her shoulders.

"Push me now, Mommy," the younger daughter said, but the other little girl was complaining, "No, do me more!"

The woman continued pushing the older girl for a while, then went to the younger. She pushed mechanically as if there were no joy, only obligation, in what she was doing.

Finally she let the two swings settle, and the girls ran over to play at the edge of a small pond. After a while they came back. "Mommy, can we go swimming?" they yelled in unison.

The woman, who had been staring out over the water from her seat at a picnic table, didn't seem to be listening, so they kept yelling for a minute.

Eventually she forced herself back to awareness. "No," she said vacantly, "no."

"Why not?" the smallest girl demanded to know. "Daddy used to take us swimming."

"Mommy doesn't swim as well as Daddy did," the woman replied. Her eyes were not focused on her children at all, but on blank sky behind the pond.

"Are we going to have another daddy soon?" the girl persisted. "So we can go swimming again?"

"What?" her mother asked. She was letting her attention wander once more.

"I want to go swimming," the girl implored.

Her mother got up and began walking away, almost as though her children were not hers. "Another daddy," she was saying to herself, "another daddy."

They were going into town to buy some supplies. "Beef stew," Randy said. "No more spaghetti. And some chocolate pudding, in those plastic containers."

"Plastic spoons," Gates said. "And baby food."

"Baby food?" Both he and Randy gaped.

Gates explained: "A guy buying hair dye is an oddity. A guy buying hair dye and baby food is buying for his wife and kid. Nothing odd about that at all."

He added baby food to their list.

"Three kinds of dye is weird, though," Randy put in.

"Right,"Gates came back. "Buy two kinds in one store, the third in another, a drugstore."

"Shouldn't we wait on the hair dye till we know more? All anyone has on us is the make of the car." He was still grabbing at the hope that they were in the clear.

"A cheap pair of scissors, from the drugstore too." Gates' methodical brain was relentlessly in gear. "Aspirin for me. A big bottle. And sun tan lotion. We'll go separately, and we'll set time limits. Everybody does such and such by a certain deadline. If you're not back pronto, the other two will leave and come back half an hour later. If you're not there then, it's goodbye forever. You're on your own."

"You're jumping to a lot of conclusions," James said. "We're just going to be seen as some guys passing through town."

"Especially if we're careful," Gates said.

Two hours later they were heading back from town, paper bags in the back seat. Gates was smoldering, interrogating Randy, who'd come on to a woman in the drugstore. "I suppose you asked her what she knew about the bombing too," he prompted.

"I just worked it into the conversation," Randy said, "after we talked about what her favorite TV show was."

Gates' upper lip tightened. "That seems like a natural transition to you, does it? Sit-coms to bombs on campuses? Shit!"

"Hey, get off my back!" Randy said. "She was cute."

"You could marry her from prison!" Gates voice rasped.

By then they were pulling into the farmyard, and Randy pulled up by the house so they could unload. He was reaching to shut off the ignition of the wagon, when the six o'clock news came on. The FBI was issuing a warrant for Randy's arrest. They were investigating the involvement of at least one other individual as an accomplice.

When the newscaster shifted to another story, Randy turned down the volume. Instead of showing nervousness, he was almost proud. "Well," he laughed, "it looks like yours truly is gonna be a household word."

Gates, in the front seat, looked back to him, behind Randy. Their eyes conveyed mutual understanding, that there was a side to Randy that neither of them knew fully until then. They were going to have to deal with it.

Carrying the groceries into the house, James felt the wildness of deep fear for the first time. Was his world about to fall apart? Everything he had known—school, Beth, Harris Point—was it about to be removed? What would be left?

Gates must have been feeling something like that too. "Everything depends on that cop not making connections," he said. "Let's hope he had a fight with a credit card company, or something got him distracted after dealing with us." Taking charge fully, he told James to plan on at least one more day at the farm, at the least.

With his emotions as taut as they were, he was glad to let the tall veteran take control, to put his trust in him.

He slept solidly for a change, the whole night, from exhaustion, he knew. Yet he woke knowing that back on campus today Beth would call him, anticipating their getting together.

He'd go to Gates, he told himself, and persuade him that a telephone call wouldn't hurt. It was minimal risk, and as he said before, not calling would seem suspicious.

Oh, the demands he was making on her! How much more could she tolerate? First he'd played lunatic, then penitent supplicant, and now absentee fiancé. Mad Hamlet in the eyes of distraught Ophelia. She was always good at identifying his emotional states, but this last rash of them was beyond fathoming. Yes, how much more could she take?

Gates came up to him as he was drawing water from the well, to boil for coffee. They talked about the call to Beth, not being able to resolve anything. Then Gates hung at his side.

"You've got to get over this, you know," he said.

"Pardon?" He was surprised that Gates was initiating a conversation.

"I said you've got to get over this. You can't let it get to you like you're doing."

He felt grateful for Gates's concern, but he didn't quite know how to reply, so he stood there mute.

"Are you afraid of being caught? Is that it?"

He shook his head no, then changed his mind: "Of course that's part of it. I never thought of myself as a criminal till now."

"But it's that man we killed—that's where you're really having trouble coping." Gates waited to be agreed with.

He nodded. "I never dreamed it would turn out this way. The only thing I ever killed in my life was a hurt sparrow, when I was young and ran over it with my bike."

Gates took in the story then brought them back to the present. "It's good you feel the way you do about that man who got caught in the building."

"That's too easy an answer," he broke in. "Why should his life be taken?"

Gates started to talk but then digested what James was saying. "No answer for that. I wish I had one. You've got to put everything into a larger perspective."

"Oh, sure, Vietnam. Are we any better than the government? We kill too."

Gates let a reflective moment pass. "You've never had to watch a whole village go up in smoke in a couple of minutes. Bombs coming in over the tree line, people frantic to get out of their way. Houses torched into tinder. All of that in the name of some stupid policy made on the other side of the world. Burning flesh stinks real bad."

"I know about all that."

"You know *about* it," Gates corrected. "You don't *know* it. Not until you see some innocent peasant woman weeping over a dead husband. Not until you see rice being taken and just burnt up, while hungry kids watch."

"How long were you over there?"

"Two tours. Not quite two, actually."

They were interrupted at that moment by Randy, who'd come out onto the porch. "Well," he said, "the boy-philosopher has lowered himself to pumping water."

Gates looked up, annoyed. "For your coffee," he said to Randy, "unless you'd like to do it yourself."

Randy moved to the edge of the porch into the sun, removing his shirt, and ignoring Gates' rejoinder. "Real nice day, isn't it?" he said. "We should have bought more sun-tan oil."

Escape Route, May 1970

"Maybe you can't get over it, ever."

"Pardon?" He looked up from his reading to see Gates standing a couple of yards away. They were on the ridge, early afternoon, where he was reading, and his fellow traveler was talking—but to him or the unanswering landscape at the foot of the ridge, he wasn't quite sure. For someone who seemed to ration his words, maybe by the week, this second attempt of the day to talk about non-practical matters came as a real surprise.

"What I told you this morning, that you'd have to get over that man dying, maybe it's not possible."

Gates seemed to be pondering more, and James had the sense to let him mull, to give him momentary, respectful silence.

"The army trained me to not think of what I was trained to do—soldiers can't be soldiers and think. But they didn't train us to live with our memories. Too expensive probably, and besides, the Defense Department would have to deal with emotions. No way."

"I'm sorry you had to go through all that."

Gates may have heard him, or he may have been deaf to his reply. "The hardest part," he said, "wasn't firefights. It was counter-intelligence. We had to shoot an old man one night, a spy, we were told. Guy looked about a hundred year's old, and we told the ARVN advisor who told us to do it, it was a mistake."

He'd been standing. Now he squatted, squinting toward something he'd seen on the horizon.

"None of us wanted any part of it, that pathetic scene. We went away from the hut and drew straws. Came back and found his wife with him, pleading. Took the wife away. Followed orders.

"The next day the ARVN advisor vanished.

"I was the short straw.

"No, you probably can't get over it," he finished.

Near dusk Randy came out of the barn, where he'd been listening to the radio. "Well," he announced energetically, "we're all in this together. The cop made the connection."

James' first thought was that maybe it was natural for Randy to be upbeat since he now had two comrades in crime. Then the thought of him being an official fugitive sank in. So unjust! he thought. He was a criminal because he had a conscience. *If I were see-no-evil blind and deliberately ignorant, I'd be in no trouble at all.*

Gates didn't let him get preoccupied, though. "Okay," he said, "let's make some more decisions. First do we stay here awhile or move on? The feds will assume we've been on the move right along, on our way to Canada. So let's stay here another day at least—try to throw off their timing. Then we go west, the Coast even, or through Banff maybe. Not our original route anyway."

Both he and Randy were shaking their heads in agreement.

"Okay," Gates went on, "are we going all the way together or separately? For me it's strength in numbers. When we get closer to the border that may change."

Again Randy and he nodded assent.

"Money. How much do we have?"

Randy told them to sit tight. He left the kitchen and came back with a wad of bills as big as a baseball. As though performing, he peeled off five hundred for each of them. "I'll keep two thousand in reserve," he said, "in case the station wagon breaks down."

James was about to ask if Randy always carried that much money around, which seemed like a fortune, when he realized his fellow Harris Point native had large-bill currency he treated like pennies. Randy's dad must have really piled in a fortune when they were in high school.

Gates was still working through another of his mental check-lists. "Okay, the fake ID's are in the wagon's glove compartment."

"If we'd only had them when the cop stopped us," James lamented aloud.

"The names wouldn't have squared with the license registration," Gates countered. "The cop would have suspected car theft. Anyway, start thinking of the new person you'll be. Make up facts easy to remember. We'll need to start calling each other by our new names, so it becomes second nature in public." He took a breath. "In the morning we'll do hair. Who's cooking tonight?" It was clear that he was going to be leader for them from here on. Even Randy, who always craved being in control, was giving him an admiring go-ahead.

You'll need a new identity, Gates said, so he was fabricating a new life to go with the name he took from the forged ID. He thought maybe he'd be an architectural draftsman. Single. With an apartment in the suburbs. On a trip to see high school friends in Denver, maybe.

But the real new identity was the one he'd now taken on: fugitive, criminal, outlaw on the loose. He'd never had to look over his shoulder, second-guess, think before every action, calculate what he'd do in relation to someone doing something else, read someone's gesture to see if the person might be looking at him with suspicion. He'd started to think in those terms already, even though they were having no contact with the outside world.

The phone call to Beth was out of the question. Instead he planned to write her a long letter this morning, only to remember that letters had postmarks, which were traceable. No, part of being this fugitive would mean cutting himself off from those whom he loved, trading that life for fleeting conversation with anonymous nobodies. Or maybe he'd become confidant-friendly with shady types normally shunned, larceny experts, adroit thieves, or whatever.

He was thinking differently, and he hated it.

They did a round-robin of cutting each other's hair shorter. They decided too short a cut would look funny, given the long hair in fashion, so they opted for severe trims.

Randy joked through the whole cut that he was on his way to becoming a corporate exec. When it was James' turn he fell back into morose musing. Seeing his hair fall, he was reminded of the frailty of body parts. In an explosion, he wondered, would hair loosen before severed arms and legs flew? Was the man they'd killed conscious at all before he died. Had his hair been on fire?

After the cuts, they got out the dyes. Randy became blond, Gates became a bit of a dark-haired gypsy, and he acquired a reddish tint.

As they were finishing, Randy came in from the barn. "Hey, here's the latest," he announced. "My dad's already accused the government of planting evidence. Good ol' pops! James, your dad's disowned you."

"What? Disowned me?"

"Going through some big trauma," Randy hee-hawed. "He's called you a traitor, said the family wanted nothing more to do with you, and read from a new will he had a lawyer draw up. You're cut off forever. Pretty weird shit. Was he always like this?"

"No, just the last couple of years. Was my mother there with him?" He was sorting emotions while sifting information. He resented Randy treating his dad like a boob but felt saddened, knowing his mother was probably excluded from his dad's decision-making.

"Nope. Hey, Gates, the feds and the newshounds can't find out anything about you. They're trying like crazy to find your folks."

"None to find," Gates said softly. "My dad deserted us when I was five. My mother died of cancer when I was sixteen."

He felt an instant sympathy for Gates, at hearing this, but Randy took the information as an opportunity for crowing: "So the feds are on a wild goose chase, huh? Ya gotta love it."

He felt like bringing Randy back to seriousness, hopeless as the idea seemed. "What about the funeral?"

It was Gates who answered, who'd been listening to the radio an hour earlier. "Services are tomorrow. Washington's been pressing the widow to vindicate the war, through the husband's death. So far she's saying nothing."

Amazing, he thought, with the well-source of bitterness the wife must be carrying! She was learning a new identity too, that of widow. This morning again, she got up, half expecting to find her husband there at breakfast. Then she had to remind herself he was gone, and would be gone every day hence. If he, James, here in this semi-wilderness, was having to learn a life of caution, she was learning a life full of loss.

Loss. What if he had to think of never seeing Beth again? Or his parents? Wendy?

But that was the reality. He was starting his days with reminders too. Yet he had hope. Some day the war would end, people would see its idiocy, there would be a general amnesty for conscientious objectors who fled to Canada, and for people like himself who fell over a precipice into criminal folly.

James, James! he told himself. *Stop this ridiculous fantasy! You are an intelligent, thinking being who deserves not to deceive yourself.* He yearned to, all the same.

It was his turn with the radio two hours later. There in the barn he heard the repeat broadcast of his father, announcing that the family lawyer had written a new will for him, stipulating his son would never receive a dime of the family's wealth.

When a reporter asked if he would change his mind if his son gave himself up, Ralph Brandes said fervently that his actions were irrev—irrevok—. But he didn't know how to say the word *irrevocable.* Poor Dad, he thought, I wish you'd had the opportunity to go to college, as I had. Maybe Wendy won't disappoint you.

Another reporter asked why his wife wasn't present, and his dad said she was shy about the press. The reporter asked if his wife agreed with him, and his father said he didn't know. "You mean you didn't consult her?" he was asked. His dad got all flustered then, and James thought of the time in their Harris Point driveway, when his father charged him with being a disciple of Gene Fitzgerald. This day's broadcast was a pathetic encore of Ralph Brandes having to slink away.

You probably didn't consult Mom, he thought sadly. *You just assumed.* And Mom would be spending a lot of time with Pastor Allen these days, finding consoling Biblical passages. Well, that was fine for her. As for himself, no orthodox god seemed on the horizon with answers for him. If anything a devil was hop-scotching through the universe.

The newscast ended by saying that all friends of the bombers were being interviewed. *Interrogated*, he said back to the radio, as though it made any difference. "Friends" meant Frank and probably most of the people of conscience on campus who formerly manned anti-draft tables. It included all of the people, too, who worked in the Moratorium projects. Here was something more from the government to stick in their craws.

Beth also. Beth. Her name had become a hounding word in his head. Beth.

The FBI would have interviewed her two, three—five, six?—times, and she'd have been compliant and polite, and then pestered, on edge, with the authorities. She had grit, deep down, and would start to get smart-mouthed with the agents, who would resent her attitude and start hinting that she knew more than she was saying. Then she'd back off under the police pressure and start to resent him.

That was good in a way. She'd have to forget him eventually, and the resentment would give her a start, a reason to draw away. By now she would have begun to think of him differently.

It was a small droning sound that turned to an immense and howling roar, and it shot them out of their early daylight sleep.

"What is it?" He bolted to the kitchen window where he thought he could see better.

Randy, groggy, was stumbling toward the outside, and Gates, fuzzy eyed but functioning, was telling Randy not to leave the porch. In a second Gates joined him at the window.

When the roaring sound came back, right over the house, they both ducked out of instinct, even though they knew it was only a sound shock-wave hitting them.

"Not a chopper!"Gates pronounced.

"They couldn't know we're here!" he said, but then the plane made another pass over the roof, and he, and even Gates, panicked. "What do you see?" he shouted to Randy, while Gates, now a hundred percent awake, sprinted upstairs to get a better view.

Randy called out that he couldn't tell anything.

"Anybody on the road?" Gates called back outside, but before Randy could answer the drone crescendoed. The house shook as whatever was above them flew past yet again.

Inside, James ran from window to window. He felt cornered, like a mouse being eyed by a hovering cat. There was nowhere to hide, and any moment federal agents would appear, having surrounded the house. It was useless to try to escape, but maybe there was an odd chance the three of them could get to one of the cars, without being shot, so they could make a run for it.

They found themselves at the kitchen door, suddenly confronting silence. The plane seemed gone. Then came an odd, noxious smell.

Randy did a fifty yard dash to the ridge, over its crest. Then Gates and he heard Randy's high-pitched hilarity as he came back into view. He was calling to them exuberantly.

"Crop dusting!" he yelled. "The next farm over."

"Are you sure?" he and Gates said in unison. They were beginning to feel tensions spring away as they spoke.

"Go look for yourself. Or just breathe, for chrissakes!"

The herbicide stench was becoming stronger, and they went outside. A chemical haze was evident in the sunlight to their east.

They let fear loose in an erupting, surging joy. They couldn't stop it, and they let it overtake them. Anyone looking on, he thought, would have seen them as school boys out of control.

"Pesticides!" Randy managed to squeal out between hysteric whoops. "I love it!"

"A Piper Cub!" Gates hiccupped. And a whole new wave of silliness started.

They felt invulnerable and wonderful, for the time being.

They started out two hours later, heading west and then slightly south, keeping religiously to the speed limits. They got food from grocery stores and gas stations, one of them going in at each stop, for supplies for all of them. They wore respectable clothes they bought at a Goodwill store, and the Chevy station wagon, their backup car, ran steadily.

They slept out under the stars the first night, on the edge of South Dakota. There, the open sky seemed to stretch with nothing but hope in it.

Then Randy blundered again, the next day.

Risking exposure but craving a change of diet, they'd gone in a roadside tavern for hamburgers and a beer. No sooner inside, Randy had gotten into a conversation with two guys at the bar, who were half-drunk. They were in work clothes and arguing in a friendly way with each other.

"Naw, it's revolutionaries from outta the country," the heavier man was saying.

"Who says?" his companion countered. "I say it's the lazy college kids. Put 'em in the service and they'd straighten up—I mean out. In a hurry." He burped heavily.

"Nope. 'S people from the outside," the first man repeated.

"Huh-un!"

"Outsiders!" The first man's face was getting red, but he broke into a laugh as he slapped the counter. He was swivelling on his bar stool.

He noticed Randy on his second swivel, leaning back to his friend who was cheesy-smiled happy now too. "Hey," he said, nudging his friend in the ribs, "les ask these guys." He grinned at Randy as though he'd found a pot of gold. Randy was grinning back.

"Okay," he continued, "these uh…revo—revo—"

"–loozhunaries," his friend slurred out.

"Right! I say they're from outta the country, and my friend here says huh-uh."

Randy didn't let the man finish. He leaned toward the pair, winking broadly, saying: "You hear about the famous bombing this week?" He named their school. "Well, I'm one of the guys who did it. I'm a radical, see? I'm headed cross-country to blow up things. Starting with a cherry bomb in the toilet back there."

The larger drunk man looked at him quizzically for two seconds. Then he burst into a staccato of laughs mixed with coughing. "Hey, that's rich! That's really good!" He turned back to his friend. "Jesus, that's good! Hey, les buy these guys a beer."

His friend took a minute, letting his eyes coordinate their focus. "Gotta get back t' work, Al."

"Aw, one more."

"Nope. C'mon." And then they shook hands with Randy as they staggered outside.

Fifteen minutes later the station wagon reverberated with Gates' rebuke to Randy. "It was another dumb thing to do, Jerk!"

"But I haven't had any fun lately," Randy said back.

"Fun?" Gates exploded. "You're a fugitive!"

"Who gives a shit?"

"I do, we do," Gates hammered. "Think, for god's sakes. Stop doing these wild things!"

"Maybe," Randy said sourly, almost pouting.

Don't be bitter, he remembered telling himself a year before, don't be bitter. But oh, all the resentment that was boiling up in him from nowhere! Yesterday it was there when the crop-duster plane disappeared, after the almost euphoric realization that it wasn't federal agents searching for them. Past the elation came the feeling, burning into him, that he'd always have to be on guard, constantly, relentlessly. He'd never be able to relax; no, he'd be hounded by people pursuing him.

His mind was full of peevish resentment. Like campus radicals, for the past twenty-four hours he'd started to nurse a perverse irritation against small-time authorities, the cop who'd pulled them over for speeding, the National Guardsmen who loped over the university grounds, the petty tyrants on draft boards who fingered Howard's name on a list.

He was reserving a special loathing for them, the faceless underlings of Washington, who set in motion the hideous folly of the war. Before, he thought they were just misguided theorists, inept judges of foreign events. At this moment he was seeing them, and the president too, as men who made a game of divorcing themselves from their policy catastrophes. Men took bullets in their chests in foreign lands, and the greatest concern in the Capitol was deflecting attention from body bags being delivered to Harris Points all over the U.S. Bombs fell on innocent civilians across the world, while they sipped expensive liquors in swank cocktail lounges. Bottoms up, fellow bastards!

He imagined himself seizing them, shaking them, tightening their ties like nooses till they faced the consequences of their acts. He would tighten, their cheeks would swell to bursting, and then they would gasp, Yes, please, we understand now, please! We admit! We beg forgiveness!

The president! His face had become a mix of two, the hound dog stupidity of Johnson in a shadow behind the pitiless sockets of the present office-holder. *Office-holder! Lie-teller*! *Psychotic megalomanic*! *Let us rise*, he heard himself raging in his chest, *while the band plays "Hail to the Chief," the Chief Mocker of all Decency, no different in the back of a limousine than a sweaty Mafia boss. Step out into the sunlight, and let history see you as the nation's abscess, the pus oozing from your suit pockets.*

Stop thinking like this, James. This isn't you but someone in your body till you come to your senses. Think of Beth and those whom you hold dear.

He already felt as sorry for her as anyone could, he thought, but then he saw her being mobbed by reporters. Her husband in her past now, she was holding a press conference in front of the apartment where she lived.

They'd stopped for gas, and he went into pay. As he was standing in line, he saw her on the TV monitor above the cash register. Camera flashes were causing the woman to flinch, microphones were being thrust into her face, and behind her an audio boom looked as though it might strike her. She appeared under attack.

Reporters wasted no time on pleasantries: "The FBI says you think underground saboteurs set off the bomb. Is that true?"

"I never said that," the woman answered. "No."

"Do you want the death penalty for the people who killed your husband?"

The woman stood her ground: "I'm against the death penalty. The bombers didn't want my husband killed. They gave the police a warning."

"But how do you feel about them?"

The woman was showing tough poise, not letting herself be baited. "My husband supported us through his military research. I can't bring him back. But the war itself was partly to blame for his death."

He had to turn away from the TV then, and leave, having paid for the gas. He couldn't appear too interested in the press conference without arousing suspicion.

He had to restrain himself from running to the car, to tell his companions that the widow was amazing, that she understood about the war and about them. But he desperately wanted to run, from the excitement he was feeling.

They were spending one last day together, in a cabin in the Rockies. It was drizzling, and the water running off the eaves cascaded down. In the ash gray light of the afternoon, the green of the pine trees took on an extra richness, the boughs glistening with rain beads.

Randy was in one of the cabin's bedrooms, tuned in to rock music on the crude transistor radio they bought in Boise. Its battery weak, the signal would come and go annoyingly. Finally, James shut the bedroom door.

He made some tea for himself and Gates, who was going over maps and downing aspirin as he added milk to his cup, turning the liquid into an English concoction. "Dairy stuff for coating the stomach," he explained. "Saves the lining."

"Do you have pain round the clock?" He'd wanted to broach the subject before but never found the right opportunity.

"Most of the time."

"And it's from the shrapnel they couldn't get out?"

Most of it they did," Gates drawled. "But when the rest showed up it was too late. I'd run out of doctors."

"But the army was obligated to treat you."

Gates stirred the tea elaborately. "More complicated than that. I'd been separated by then."

"But veterans are entitled to things."

"Dishonorable discharge. No access to treatment."

"But you'd gotten a medal, you told me."

Gates sipped the hot tea cautiously. He looked out the window, at the rain, as he talked the longest he ever had. "You have to understand. The last months I was there, in Nam, it had all gone bad—hamlets taken, falling back into enemy hands, taken again, falling again. Nobody we could trust in the friendly forces. Good officers exhausted, hospital cases. Washington babbling victory, grunts on dope all the time.

"One day this squeaky voice lieutenant shows up, tells us to hit such and such.

"We'd been there three days before, knew the terrain, swamp and paddies with one narrow way in and out. Barely got out, with heavy losses. Only three of us came back.

"'Have to take the objective,'" the little snot said. "Fresh from officer training, been in country two weeks. Then Mister Squeaky says we don't have the guts for going in there!

"My buddy, Aldaz, is looking at the end of his tour in ten days. Going home versus going back in. Going crazy. He went even crazier when the snot said what he did. By then I'd told the lieutenant to use our orders in the latrine.

"Two hours later, Squeaky's out of action himself, fragged by Aldaz, who was desperate. You know what fragging is?"

He nodded. The stories of rebellious troops killing superiors were on the evening news the previous autumn.

Gates was gulping his tea now, hot as it still was, steaming steadily. He seemed ready to let the narrative end, but he turned his look away from the rain, back inside, while facing him, expecting James to respond.

He guessed at a proper reply: "Some other officer came to order you back in?"

"No," Gates shook his head. "Aldaz and I were court-martialed. Too many people overheard our little discussion with The Squeak."

"Jesus, Steve!"

Gates did another of his shrugs. "Couldn't blame the military in a way. Their business is having people obey orders. I just didn't realize a dishonorable discharge cut off my medical treatment." He took a large gulp of tea, the liquid so seemingly hot it might have been scalding. "Back home, the pain came back. I asked for an appeal of the court-martial decision. By then I was a non-person to Uncle Sam."

Gates turned to gaze at the drizzle outside again, a long absorbed look. James could only ponder the anger that he had lived through, was living through every day. No wonder he was a willing participant in this thing they'd done. And his pain, that in the stomach, was only a fraction of what he must have dealt with daily.

He knew it would happen but not as quickly. He was forgetting Beth already. Fight the phenomenon as he wanted to, it was occurring. In the process his helplessness dissolved into sadness. If only he'd taken the picture of her that he kept on the dresser in his room. Maybe then he could remember all the things he wanted to remember.

He could recall the color of her hair, the occasional fierceness of her sarcasm, the way she breathed on the pillow. But he'd forgotten the color of her eyes, and what she wore the last time they were together. Clothes were unimportant, he knew; still, clothes were part of images, which were part of memories, and the memories were slipping away like spilled mercury.

Was he worrying the memories to death? Maybe, he told himself, he should just relax and let her conjured self reappear.

He knew the mind-trick being played on him. He felt guilt, and with that came denial. If he no longer had a picture of her, then he no longer had to deal with what he'd done to her. How convenient, except that he loved her, deeply wanted her to be beside him now. If only she weren't so faceless all of a sudden!

He could imagine his dad, starkly seeing him as his new father, the no-nonsense patriot. What a sad end his son had brought the man to. But his dad would have American righteousness to see him through, never mind that the righteousness had a hollow core.

His mother would be a shambles whose faith might see her to a livable if diminished life, and if the church beacon burned less intensely as a refuge light, there would be his sister. Wendy, he comforted himself, was someone coming into her own lately, a person rising to the demands of these wretched days. She'd know somehow, how to steer his mother through the wreckage. Oh, he could remember his family vividly. But Beth…?

Randy pulled the car under a shade tree in the small town, while he and Gates got out. They took their backpacks from the trunk and came round front again.

Randy had the same self-confident look he always had. On a shoestring cord he was breezily twirling a small good-luck charm, a plastic frog that croaked "Hi!"

"Be careful," James cautioned as they shook hands. "We'll see you in a month."

"Just be cool in Customs,"Gates added. "The Canadians probably won't check you. They'll just wave you through."

"Happy hitchhiking,"Randy replied. "Get some dirt on your faces. You look too clean-cut."

"One of us may even pass you, if we get a lucky lift," he said.

The two of them watched Randy drive away, the station wagon banking at the turn a half-mile down the road.

Close to the border, they'd all decided to go separate ways. What Gates and he hadn't told Randy was that only Randy was going on to Canada. They were turning south.

"I feel like a betrayer," he said to Gates. "We go back a long way, in Harris Point."

Gates shrugged. "Randy didn't tell you what we were really going to do to Horton Hall. Just remember that."

"I know." But he didn't feel much conviction in what he said.

"It's self-survival," Gates pressed. "You and I both know he's going to get himself caught."

He couldn't argue with that at all. The two of them had based their decision on that when they talked privately the day before. There was no point in their making the arrest a three-some spectacle, they figured.

They themselves were splitting, only for the present. Later, they would get back together.

He liked Gates by now, respecting his candor and intelligence. He was the reason they'd gotten this far, and with a little more luck they just might elude the authorities, drift into anonymous lives somewhere and spend their days in a quiet seclusion.

He found Gates unassuming at first, humble later. He had a quiet, droll wit that came out when you got to know him. For someone without a parental past, he'd managed to find an identity he could sustain. Even now, in this new testing, the man was his own person.

At this small town park's crossroads, they discussed which routes they would go. Gates thought he would head west and then south. A bit back east and then southwest, that was his own choice.

"Well," Gates said, extending his hand. "Good luck, James. Lots of hikers on the road these days. Improves our chances."

"I don't know how to thank you," he said. He felt like he should say some kind of tribute, but Gates headed off any possibility of it. His companion picked up his bag to trudge down the street.

"Looks like a nice bit of shade down there to sit in," he said, "if I have to wait a while." He put a hand on James' shoulder, as he strode past. "You take care now."

A block away, he plunked himself on a curb, shaded by a building. Even at that distance James could see him take his small knife out of his pocket and start to clean his nails.

"Thanks," he said, though he knew he couldn't be heard. "Thanks anyway."

He watched for a half hour until a small red sedan pulled over to give Gates a lift. Then he went out to the road himself, to wait. Within fifteen minutes he had a ride from a teenager driving a panel truck.

He remembered a situation similar to this one, in which he picked up the hitchhiker who'd shop-lifted items from the grocery store near the camp where he worked. He was furious at the petty crime, and the petty criminal. Now, here he was in the hitchhiker's seat, a bomber-felon on the loose. How far back in time that was, how far back, indeed!

It was six months later, and he was walking down an obscure mountain road. The stones on the road hurt his feet, but the clear air cooled his face.

He turned right, as the old man in the little town told him to do, and walked a quarter a mile up a hill. When he got to its top he saw the small adobe house off to the left, sequestered in a group of squat, thick trees. On one side of it was a small shed, and all around it was a fence that held nothing in nor out. A dark young woman was outside, hanging up clothes. When she saw him, she slipped inside, hurriedly.

When he got to the gate, a man appeared in the doorway of the house but in the deep shadow of the roof, so he wasn't sure if it was the right person or not. He took five more steps and stopped.

Gates stepped out into the sunlight. "You made it too," he said, in his typically quiet way. But he was effusive for a change. "Congratulations, James."

"You too. Damn, it's good to see you."

Their handshakes fused, and then Gates ushered him inside. "You heard about Randy?"

"Yes. How did you know, down here I mean?"

"Short-wave radio. When we talked, you and I, we gave him—what?—ten days before he'd be captured?"

"Yes. He went sixteen."

"Sad that he got caught," Gates said. "You hear all the details coming out about the My Lai massacre, that our marines did?"

"Enough to make my conscience a lot better." In the dark of the house, his eyes were adjusting, and he saw the woman step forward. She was dark, maybe Indian. She was pregnant, slightly swollen beneath the cotton shift she wore.

"This is Maria,"Gates said. "Maria, this is James, the person I've told you about."

From the tone of her speech, from her first sentences, he knew she was a strong person. "Hello, James," she said. "We hoped you'd make it."

"I did, too," he said back, and the three of them laughed at the obviousness of their shared wish.

They sat down for the first of many meals together. Gates explained the security precautions they took, and Maria told him about the surroundings. He'd want to stay on the farm pretty much, she said, but eventually they'd introduce him to others they knew.

Later Gates showed him around the small plat they worked, and Maria helped him fix up the small back room which would be his until the baby arrived. In the late afternoon he went out to work in the fields, and once, as he leaned on his hoe, he looked back on the small adobe dwelling.

He had left behind a past life and come to terms with leaving it. Living as someone else, named James Brandes, whose government had tested a generation in ways that never occurred before, he'd responded as needed, even though that conflicted with the government, and his family and the institutions he had born into. He couldn't do anything about the past now except apply its lessons to the future.

He would choose the family of man, an abstraction hard to define. His own future would be circumscribed and narrow, but he thought he could carry on a kind of existence that would include fairness and care for others, an accumulation of small, meaningful daily acts.

He thought he would like his new surroundings since here were people who would know and trust him, and who could be trusted in return. It wasn't an ideal life, but in time it could be somewhere he would think of as home. Before him lay something like a renewed start in life.

Epilogue: Denver and Harris Point, March 1989

It happened every time he came to this city for a professional conference, roughly once every eight years.

It happened rarely enough that between times he would almost forget the events took place. However, occasionally, sitting in his university office, he would be drawn back in recollection, to this hotel, where he always stayed. Here at some time in his stay a hotel employee behind the front desk would hand him a nine-by-twelve manila envelope with his name on it: Professor John T. Oates.

He would take it and then he would carry out his clandestine mission.

Again! he thought, carefully tucking the envelope in his briefcase, as the hotel desk manager handed him the packet. Once more he would be called upon to play the role of conspirator courier.

The first time, three years after the bombing of Horton Hall, he'd received the mysterious envelope and taken it to a conference session in which he was to be part of a symposium. Then five minutes before he was supposed to hold forth brilliantly in front of his peers, he casually opened the unstamped packet, containing a smaller envelope, to Harris Point. Perplexed at first, that sensation gave way to astonishment seconds later, when he read the note to him.

John,

I need you to place the accompanying letter in the briefcase of someone at the conference who lives on the West Coast. You should insert it into the briefcase in such a way that the owner won't find the letter till arriving home. Then, presumably, the bearer will find it and mail it, as any helpful person would. If you agree to this, please acknowledge your activity by stepping outside the hotel at five o'clock today and loosening your tie at the taxi stand. After that, stroll south. No one will contact you personally.

If you feel you cannot do this, destroy everything immediately, for obvious reasons.

If you agree to help, then destroy this cover letter as soon as possible. Thanks for your small act of courage.

You are well, I trust.

I am not in this city.

James Brandes

So taken back was he that he was barely coherent during the next hour. One of his colleagues, in fact, asked him if he was running a fever, since he had missed Professor So and So's blatant point about whatever, entirely.

All he could think about, as his colleagues did verbal sparring, was that he was being asked to be a courier for a man accused of murder. Yes, of course no ordinary murderer, for this was James Brandes, who'd been drawn starry-eyed into the Horton Hall scheme apparently, but the FBI still classified him as a murderer, nonetheless.

That afternoon, so long before, he let his body govern his head. He found himself walking out of the hotel at five, loosening his tie as directed, and then strolling south. He really wasn't conscious of having thought through anything. He was just doing it.

Some stroll. He sweated, in a March wind with the temperature in the forties. Would the FBI grab him then and there? he asked himself.

Was he being set up? Perhaps the madness of the late sixties and early seventies had never really stopped. But he walked unhindered, returning to the hotel and actually sleeping soundly that night, for five hours anyway.

The next day, the last of the conference, he felt like an adventure novel spy as he saw one of his West Coast colleagues leave his briefcase unattended. It was easy to slip the letter to Harris Point into it, behind a sheaf of papers. From there it would find its way to an office in Seattle, where his fellow political scientist would become a second courier, unknown to himself, by dropping the letter into a convenient campus mailbox.

The first letter went through, he knew, because James Brandes' mother went to the FBI with it, in a vain effort to find her son. When she did federal agents crawled all over Seattle, assured from the letter's postmark that James was there and would be arrested imminently. Oates remembered the relish he felt at the news reports of the FBI chasing down false leads. For someone who had no criminal background, James Brandes was doing quite well, thank you, at buffaloing the nation's finest.

He wondered about the fate of the second letter. Evidently, it went from the briefcase of a peer into the wastebasket.

Now, this third time, he hoped James' letter would go through, to give some odd comfort, at least, to James' family.

As for himself, this routine was easier to do. By this third time now, there was a pattern to everything, and he rather enjoyed the cloak and dagger life. In his old age maybe he'd tell his grandchildren about what he was doing today.

His role was fitting, too, in a special way. The previous year he and two of his university colleagues discovered, through a suit brought by someone else under the Freedom of Information Act, that they were on a list of subversives, drawn up during the Vietnam War.

None of them could imagine what warranted their being remotely eligible for such a list. All they did was ask questions of their students, sign petitions, present papers at conferences like this one, and preside at the most non-violent of public rallies. But after the three of them found out about the list, they got the government to publish an official apology in the local papers. Along with the apology came a handsome monetary settlement he used to buy the small ketch he always wanted.

He put the manila envelope into his briefcase, to be forwarded in the usual unconventional way. Oh, he thought, if the government knew the whole story! It was a thought you could find pleasure in, yes, ironic pleasure, not to put too fine a point on the idea.

Janine Brandes went out shopping that morning, leaving Wendy and her new baby, Justin, at home. It was a standard arrangement for them: Every Saturday Wendy would open the sporting goods store, leaving young Tom Gibson in charge, and then come over for a long coffee. Today, at age sixty and a touch arthritic at times, she ran out of apple juice for the baby, so she went to FoodSource shortly after Wendy arrived.

Now she was home, but Wendy was out there in the driveway, in the rain, waiting for her. Really it was embarrassing. The neighbors would think her daughter had no common sense.

"Come in quick, Mom! Leave the groceries." Wendy was alternately pulling and shoving her. Both of them inside, her daughter made her sit down with her coat still on.

"It's James! He's written again."

Now it was her turn to act as though she had no common sense. She was out of the chair, then back in it, faint from excitement, whooping, hugging Wendy.

"It's a decade, isn't it? No, a decade and a half now! Well read it, silly! I can't with these tears in my eyes. Hurry!"

"But we need to decide something first, about—"

"Read it, Wendy, for heaven's sakes."

Wendy smoothed the letter on her skirt before she read the words.

Dear Mom and Wendy,

For reasons I can't explain I can only contact you this way, and this seldom. A letter I wrote you eight years ago never reached you, I'm sad to say.

You gave my first letter to the FBI to try to find me. I understand why you did that, but if you keep this one a secret I believe we'll all be better off.

I don't intend to turn myself in to the authorities ever. You will probably never see me again, but you should know that I have a life that gives me quiet satisfaction. I'm in good health and with people who appreciate me, as I appreciate them.

A year after Dad's heart attack I found out about his death. I think of him now as he was when I was young, before Vietnam, when he was able to just own the store and be a good husband and father.

I think of both of you often. Wendy probably has children, and maybe you have remarried, Mom. I hope so.

I'd like to describe the way I spend my days, but I can't without divulging something that would lead to my being discovered.

Being somewhat older now, almost forty, I understand what we went through in that terrible time. Maybe people will eventually come to terms with what our government set in motion. I still have the deepest sadness for having taken someone's life. Yet I remind myself of all the lives lost senselessly during that era. Maybe my act halted some of that.

Harris Point seems so far away, but you're always near.

My caring, enduring love to you both.

James

"Now, Mom, we've got to decide things," her daughter was saying, but her chest was so full of feeling she wasn't able to speak. Wendy handed her the letter, and she clutched it in her hand, tightly, thinking she might never let go of it.

When she calmed down, the two of them took less than five minutes to decide: This time they wouldn't notify the authorities.

That one time, the only other time, three years after the bombing, they did what they were supposed to. They phoned that agent Metcalf.

Oh, he was there lickety-split, taking James's letter, promising to give it back but then reneging, promising a copy but never coming through with that either. It was official evidence, he told them. He had to keep it.

Then he got her to go on TV, to make another plea to James to give himself up. The Bureau had psychological experts who were telling Metcalf and her that this was a breakthrough. James was on the verge of coming forward, and the family would have him back again, after a short jail term, of course. The FBI would change the murder charge to involuntary manslaughter.

James didn't come forward, though. And as for the jail term, Randy got thirty years! Some short term!

And as Wendy pointed out, what if Randy had implicated James as one of the bombing's planners, not just a driver of the car? Randy would go along with whatever the FBI offered, to shorten his sentence or speed up early parole. They asked Metcalf about this, but he avoided answering. They could never be sure.

Yes, it all made sense. There was no need to contact the authorities, and as a matter of fact Metcalf hadn't called her in almost a year now. He seemed to be losing interest.

There was another thing about Metcalf. The last time they had talked, she asked him if he was a religious man, and he told her that he was, he was a Mormon.

She didn't know what Mormons were like, she remembered thinking. But she was sure they weren't like her, in what they believed. They had more than one wife, the men, maybe half a dozen. Goodness! What kind of religion was that!

She didn't tell Wendy about that part of her conversation with Metcalf, and now she decided to keep it to herself still.

Wendy's baby was crying. She went to get it, to walk the floors with it while feeding it the juice she got at the store. As she walked the infant, she reread her son's letter in her free hand. Three and four more times she treasured its words.

What a morning it was! She was happier than she'd been in years.

"Justin," she said to the uncomprehending baby in her arms, "I have a son, your uncle, a good and kind man you will probably never know, who's made peace with himself."

Washington, D. C., Spring 1992

Just Mom and Dad and the two kids, one of each sex, on a Saturday afternoon, seeing the sights of the nation's capitol. Here they were on the beautiful mile of grass next to the Smithsonian, and the Hirschorn Gallery, which they had just gone to. Here she was, on this bench with the crocuses in bloom near her. "Dad" made her sit down while he went off with the kids for ice cream. He was waving to her at this moment, in the distance, too far away for his facial expression to be visible, but she knew he was looking at her with his usual affection.

Sixteen years of togetherness meant they could read each other's gestures and expressions if they were a football field away from one another.

Just Mom and Dad and the kids. At times she yearned to be that common, ordinary "Mom" person. But she knew herself well enough now, at forty-one, to know she was probably destined to end up differently. She always had too much resolve, energy, and imagination, her parents always remarked, to end up "usual."

Little did she think, though, that this was where she would end up, in Washington, D.C. Some mornings, waking in her apartment, she felt displaced. Then when she got to her office, and people started pressing her for decisions, appointments, her signature on proposals—well, at times she did feel like an imposter. The leap from her former life to this one was still requiring some adjustment, even after these first months.

Beth Stephens, Member of Congress! From Illinois, the Chicago suburbs. It was true, and she liked the sound of it, she had to admit. Her new life was exciting. Maybe even as early as high school she secretly believed she'd be somewhere like this, and it had happened. She was happy in the new role, ecstatic at times, in a way.

Frank was looking back at her. He seemed to be observing something, wary of that slouching man in sunglasses with a baseball cap, who was walking aimlessly toward her. He was hardly threatening in appearance. How could Frank be worried about him?

Her Frank. She was asking so much of him now. Her living in Washington all week and then commuting to Chicago on the late-night Thursday flight—what strains it was putting on their strong, cherished marriage. Each of them acknowledged that her election would challenge them, but neither knew the depth of what would happen, the fatigue, the loss of daily contact. Oh sure, they talked by phone every day, but it just wasn't the same as standing there next to someone after dinner, talking as the dinner table got cleared.

That man she'd known so long, she didn't know all of him, she recently found out. Frank was revealing a streak of remarkable patience and stamina, as Shaun and Heidi's caretaker. Too, his single-mindedness with tasks had given way to more spontaneity.

He had to be more flexible with the kids these days, just as she was giving up some of her closeness to those two. She resented it, hated it even, during the kids' formative years, but she had no choice. She hoped they would forgive her, and of course Frank was there, back home in Ryan's Park every day, hounding into them that she loved them. Shaun was beginning to say Frank was becoming a stupid bore about old absent Mom out there in Washington.

They were trying to keep their kids normal. Except for the swearing-in ceremony, this was the first time they'd brought the children to this city, and this weekend the whole family was roughing it, camping out in her apartment instead of in a hotel.

They wanted the kids to understand there was no special treatment for members of Congress, in the same way they always preached "no special privileges" when she was on the school board and then mayor of the city, back home.

In the distance she could see Heidi pestering her brother, something she was doing often lately. Was this the younger ten-year-old taking on the twelve-year-old elder? Frank and she thought the kids were beyond this stage, but maybe sibling friction was back again. Damn.

Who would have thought, she considered, that years ago, in college and intoxicated with grand ideas, she'd sometime have to be occupied with such tiny domestic matters? Soon, today probably, she'd have to take Heidi aside and tell her once again she was as important as her older brother. This time, though, she'd have to do a better job of it.

She shuddered a bit, recalling her college years. Those were supposed to be golden days of carefree youth, and yet for her generation it hadn't been that at all. Plus her college years had ended so horridly, with a man she loved just falling out of her life, becoming—god!—a fugitive.

For her the golden years happened five years afterward, when she found out that Frank, James' former apartment mate, had moved to the Chicago area. One Sunday morning he called out of the blue, and the next week they went out to dinner, and then there were more dinners. He was a funnier man than she remembered, more confident now, awfully creative in bed, for a scientist, and they were both wild about that old junk sports car he was restoring.

Yes, they'd survive this time, she knew. Their kids would likely turn out normal, though not too normal she hoped. After all, they needed to be individuals.

"Mind if I sit down?"

She'd been looking at Frank admiringly, still in the distance, so she didn't notice the stranger with the baseball cap, who was seating himself on her bench, fairly close to her although he could have sat further away. From a backpack he had, he was removing a book, which he opened and appeared to be reading.

She glanced back at Frank, who was acting a bit strange again, looking around the grass area as though one of the kids had run away and vanished. But both Heidi and Shaun were right there with him.

What was Frank so leery of, she wanted to know.

"Don't be frightened, Beth. I'm going to talk while I appear to be reading. You'll want to look at me, but don't look too long. When you talk, look forward, as though we're not conversing. If someone walks by, don't talk at all, okay?"

Good god, she thought, what's going on? *This absolute stranger knows my name, and he's ordering me around like he owns me. Is this some kind of kidnaping? Surely, new members of Congress aren't that important to terrorists*!

Then she recollected the voice next to her, the sound of—

"No, you're not in a science fiction movie. It's me, James. Why don't you look now, but not too long. We're probably not being watched, but I have to be careful."

His features weren't too distinct, hidden as they were by the sunglasses and cap, but when she looked she saw a familiar mouth line, jaw, and a mole by his ear. It was him!

Her breaths became so choked, it was as though her body was parceling them out, as she realized everything in a cataclysmic instant. "You and Frank set this up, didn't you?"

"Don't ask him how. If you don't know anything, you can't be prosecuted. If you want to leave, to protect your career, just get up and walk away. I'll understand."

She was beginning to get some control of her emotions and thoughts. She even came out with a tremorous laugh: "I'm just having a little trouble, uhm...dealing with.... It really is you!"

"We couldn't warn you in advance. It's wonderful your being in Congress. Your love of talking must have been a real campaign asset." She could see he was trying a little humor to set her at ease.

"Right now I'm speechless." She reminded herself to keep staring ahead, not looking at him, but it was almost impossible.

She heard a chuckle. "You're beautiful. I always imagined you would be."

"I have bags under my eyes all the time. I never get enough sleep."

"The price of wanting to change the world," he said with a tinge of resignation. "Your kids are lovely too."

"And I'm not giving them enough time these days, with me here in this boiling soup-pot city. Politics never stops here, and I've so many demands on my time. Frank's wonderful with the children. Do you have any of your own?"

"I can't tell you anything about my life. Sorry." He paused a minute. "You and Frank seem well suited to one another."

She had a thought that she started but couldn't finish: "I wish you could—No, never mind. I just had this stupid wish that the three of us could sit at our kitchen table in Ryan's Park, sharing old memories. It was silly of me to think of it."

His response didn't come quickly. "The old college times weren't such good old times, were they?" he said with obvious pain. "Frank supports your political life, does he?"

"He hated me running for Congress. He still loathes this government."

"A view I once shared," she heard. "But governments aren't immovable forever. They're just collections of people that come and go with the times. You, for instance. Did I come up as an issue in your run for national office?"

She was still reminding herself to not turn sideways, and she was getting better at it, sadly. "All the time. A reporter found out about you and me, and then it was open season on me. But young people, who had no memory of the war, began to see the opposition as one-issue fanatics. What mattered was all the school board meetings and city council sessions I'd sat through. And my getting out to neighborhoods.

One day I shook five hundred hands." She broke off abruptly. "Oh, dear, here's Beth the Talker yammering away again."

James was taking things in quietly, a touch distracted. She saw him do a momentary surveillance of the area. Then he offered an insight. "Odd, isn't it, that so much of our lives were consumed with that war, and now it seems like something that happened to our grandparents?"

"I think about it at least once a week," she told him. "If we ever, ever think about doing something like that again, I'm going to be there screaming on the House floor, reelection be damned." She let her intensity come down a bit and then revealed something else: "During the campaign, when your name first came up, I began hating you," she said. "Then one night Frank sat me down and told me what to do, to stop blaming and simply say that the war was a mistake, that you were a victim of circumstances, and that it was time to get on with the future. It was honest, and the voters liked it. And I could live with myself after that."

As she had done, now it was time for him to go the whole way back, to a university campus in the Midwest, in an era that wouldn't go away. He said, "I almost couldn't live with the pain I caused you, just having to abandon you."

She let his thought hold her a moment. "I knew that finally. After six months I grasped how you got caught up in things." She waited then suggested something: "You could probably give yourself up now, you know."

"No," he said immediately. "We lost a war, and this government won't forget that. It wouldn't treat me fairly, despite your new part and forgiving place in it."

She knew he was right, and that her suggestion was pointless. She felt infinite sadness and tenderness swelling in her. "I'd like to hold your hand," she said. "Please. Forget the risk to me."

"I'd better not," she heard, but within a second she felt contact from his fingers. They sat there, wordless, touch bridging miles, years, experiences.

"I have to go," he said finally. "Frank's going to be coming this way." He faced her directly, removing his sunglasses as he swung sideways. "I'm happy for you, your new life."

She couldn't breathe well again, taking in his features, which looked so old and yet youthful in a way. Then she got out more words somehow. "In the campaign the reporters and the opposition somehow missed a fact. It might have destroyed me."

"Yes?" He was putting away his book, ready to get on his feet.

"When Frank and I had our son, we did something we never regretted."

"Shaun, is that his name?" he asked.

"Not just Shaun. Shaun James. It was Frank's idea, and it took me one tenth of a second to agree."

He was standing now, about to walk away. "Shaun James," he repeated, simultaneously talking away from her and to her. "You didn't have to do that."

"We've think it's one of the best things we've done in our whole lives," she said resolutely.

He hesitated as though weighing options: "Before, when I said that I couldn't tell you anything, well let's say I'm not alone. There's a woman...like you in a way...strong."

"As gentle and caring as you, James?"she prompted. But then she could see him tensing, being on guard again, and she knew he had to retreat, to go back being a mystery for his own good. "I'm happy for you too," she added, feeling inadequate with her words. She sensed they were the last ones she would ever say to him, and knowing they were, she felt her throat tightening.

Briefly, he turned to her, for a parting look. Their eyes said everything, and then he turned and strolled away, gone from all the rest of her days.

She sat there a moment, seeing Frank coming toward her. No, she told herself, he would never be fully gone from the shadowed places of their hearts. This man James Brandes—college friend and lover, reluctant revolutionary, obscure human wanderer—was lodged there in that enduring richness called sorrow.

Author's Note

I wrote the first version of "Events of the Day" shortly after the bombing of Sterling Hall on the University of Wisconsin Campus in Madison, in 1970. Then I abandoned the manuscript till I found it in a box in the attic, decades later, after the Gulf War.

By then, older and more interested in history, I took up the work again with enthusiasm.

Although the novel began as a reaction to a local event, I resisted giving Madison's place-name to later versions of the story since I didn't want to reduce it to a chronicle of a known, sensational crime. Tom Bates had already exhausted that material, in rich detail, in his non-fiction book "Rads"(Harper Collins, 1992). Instead I went in search of larger messages: what The Sixties were like for common Midwesterners, what the Vietnam war meant and how it lingered in the moral consciousness of a generation.

As a historical novelist, I mainly kept the chronology of the war intact. However, I did change the facts of the campus unrest and violence, at times, for fictional drama. The anti-Dow protest actually happened in 1968, not 1969, and the math building bombing occurred in August rather than May of 1970.

I saw no need, either, to make any of my bomber characters like those in real life. James Brandes, my central character, bears no resemblance to Karlton Armstrong or the other "New Year's Gang" members.

Trying to capture The Sixties is a tricky task, and I had to eliminate or pare down some historical developments in favor of others. Feminism gained more momentum during the era than I have shown, although Beth is very much a Sixties' product late in the book, I think. Mysticism and interest in the cosmos was stronger on campus than I portrayed. On campus and off, communal living enjoyed a revival, but in "Events of the Day" it barely exists.

Language usage changed dramatically during The Sixties, when radicals used obscenity as a political weapon and radical speech was taken up as an everyday facet of a jaded life-style. But that trend toward outrageous talk caused a major problem, which I wrestled with unsuccessfully.

How many times can a person say "Fuck you!" and still have the word convey meaningful shock?

Although "fuck"had shock value in the sixties, by the mid-Nineties that word and its obscene cousins were so commonplace, they carried no impact whatsoever. FuckYouSpeak was just mannered, lazy talk, often generated by Hollywood producers to rev up innocent teens, in their zeal for box office.

What to do? Use "fuck" every other sentence, as a set of Spike Lee's characters once did? Ho-hum. Yawn.

Create a brand-new obscene language my characters would speak? Impossible to do, though to any lover of language, like me, the prospects were tantalizing.

In the end I sanitized the way my people spoke. Better that they talk as real people of today at least, I reasoned, rather than as caricatured, cartoony leftists of the Vietnam era.

Too often that time is portrayed as a wild, decade-long protest party by the young or as a grand plot by Washingtonians who would later become charter members of Megalomaniacs Anonymous. It was a little bit of each of those, but in the end it was a tragic time involving much more.

If I brought back the morality of the era I succeeded.

9 780595 010707